HARECLOUGH HEIGHTS

BARRY THOMAS

DEDICATION

To my whole family, whom I love dearly.

ACKNOWLEDGEMENT

Thank you, Georgi James
For your help and encouragement.

Contents

Chapter 1

HISTORY

The highest road overlooking our town of Hareclough was aptly named Hareclough Heights.

My name is Martin Daniels, I was named after my Granddad, and I have just celebrated my 18th birthday.

I am sitting on one of the many memorial benches scattered across the hill, where you can see everything as one perfect vista.

This bench was dedicated to my grandad by the family.

He was Captain Martin Daniels, well known in the area as Captain Daniels, following his heroism in the First World War.

He would lead the Remembrance Day parade every November, wearing the row of medals he had been given during that war.

When I was growing up, I used to help him polish them.

"One day, Martin, you will own my medals and be able to wear them with pride

at the cenotaph when I am gone."

I dreaded that day as it would mean my granddad had passed away.

Central to the picture is the 15th-century church with its spire reaching towards the cloud as if to give those heading from the church to heaven a shortcut.

History tells us that the church was first built as a wooden structure, which burned down in the early 1400s.

It was rebuilt in stone and remained perfect until King Henry VIII decided to have its roof removed during his reformation period.

It soon fell into poor repair, and as it collapsed, a lot of its stones were taken to build houses or repair fallen farmers' walls, which in turn were also taken to make something else.

The footing stones remained, and the present church was built in the 1700s, with additions made in the centuries that followed.

From up here, you see the grounds surrounding the church, and its gravestones resemble shuffled dominoes standing on their ends, some fallen over.

Although we are far away from the church here, the squeak of the large iron gates can be heard when they are opened or closed, carried on the breeze.

I think one of the gravestones dates to the mid-1400s and was for one of the first Ministers in the parish.

The river Tauper disappears in each direction as you view down from our seat.

It is very popular in the summer and offers a wide range of water sports, all of which are available from the old boathouse.

The old boathouse was always referred to as such from the day it was built.

Carvings into the header stone read, The Old Boat House 1920

Some confusion about whether it was built after one had fallen, and who would call a new building the Old Boat House?

In 4 or 5 places along the river, you will see fine golden sands fringed with some shingle— a magnet for the younger families with lots of free parking behind the river and beach.

In each car park is a toilet block and some form of refreshments, all have the ice cream van playing its ' stop me and buy one' theme at regular intervals.

Over the years, it has proven to be an excellent fishing river, with both salmon and trout. The saying goes, it takes a good angler to catch some trout, but it takes a lucky angler to catch a salmon.

The visitors can buy a full day's angling pass from the boat house; there is a limit to how many fish you can take out in a day. I personally think that is to trick the fishermen into a false sense of great fishing.

Diligence is always needed as the river Tauper can change from a Lamb to a Lion in moments, especially if it rains hard upstream.

If it had rained, you could see the excess water rushing down, flooding the riverbanks and carrying all manner of debris in its wake.

Over the years, the River Tauper has claimed many lives.

Some are very tragic accidents, and others are not!

I live just opposite that piece of open land just before the car parks start.

The sandy beach on this side is ours; I live in the left-hand house behind it with my dad, Brian, and mum, Alice.

My mum and dad built the house and the one next door after a bequest from the owner of Hareclough House at that time. My dad and grandad fought with him during the war, and he never forgot their bravery.

In Hareclough, we have three bridges spanning the river, one a 1900s iron bridge that carries the busy railway line, serving both freight, tourists, and commuters.

The new school, Hareclough High School, covered a big area to the right of the church. Also on its grounds were the nursery, infant, and junior schools.

They had their own entrance, separate from the high school's, mainly for the safety of the youngsters when school started and finished.

It has always been called the new school, even though it was built in Victorian times on an ancient burial ground.

It was not so crucial in 1876, but nowadays, if a householder digs over a garden, the archaeological crew are upon them.

Big plans were already afoot for our school`s 150th anniversary.

A whole week of bands, kiddies' races and games, Bingo Nights, Whist Drives, culminating in a dance with two groups on, one local and the other one a surprise.

The doubters amongst us would think it was a surprise because they did not have one yet, or a surprise, as they were such a big band, and they did not want a lot of off-cumdens filling the large school hall.

I was one of the later thinkers, hopefully.

Right next to the school was Hareclough sports ground.

The school had always used it for their outdoor activities.

I play football here on one of the three grass pitches. I am following in the footsteps of my dad and grandad, who both captained the side; hopefully, my time will come.

When I was in school, we had sports day, and we used the running track.

From start to finish, it was 400 yards.

From up here, it looks like an elongated dartboard, happy days.

On the opposite side of the valley, just behind our house, is Hareclough House, a former mansion. I think I heard it said it was Georgian; I need to research that further.

I played in the yard with the children of the staff from the house or the farm workers' children. It was a lovely and memorable time I will never forget. From about 14 years old down to the youngest child, we all played together without ever arguing. We were content and safe there.

What was I doing on the top of Hareclough Hill? I take our dog, Peggy, for a walk up here most days. She is two years old, on Sunday, as it happens, and my family has always had chocolate brown Labrador retrievers going back generations.

And strangely enough, always called them Peggy.

A long time ago, my great-grandfather used to breed Labrador Retrievers, and our Peggy is part of that first family; someone has bred them ever since.

Now our Peggy is 2, she will be the next to have some puppies, I hope, but Uncle Paul sees to all that sort of thing. He has kennels

My great-grandfather was a gamekeeper for the Hareclough House estate, and he bred

Labrador retrievers as working dogs for the shooting season.

My dad said his dogs were sold worldwide because the working breed was so strong.

They lived in the Gamekeepers' cottage on the estate; the trees hide it from where I am sitting. I think his wife, my grandma, was in service at the House.

When I get home, I will research my ancestors to create a family tree.

Then I will try to write everything I can find about them.

I hope you enjoy reading it. Today's dateline is 1992, dubbed the naughty nineties, I do hope I have not missed it.

C`mon Peggy.

Chapter 2

CAPT. DANIELS

My great-granddad was the gamekeeper for the Hareclough House estate.

My mum and dad lived and worked at Hareclough House, and so I was born there.

My mum worked as an assistant seamstress, and my father was the associate head lad.

"Just pop in and ask the cook if she has a little lard so I can soften up this new saddle the Master has just bought, please, Martin."

"Yes, straight away, father, I will run there and back. Excuse me, Cook, my father wants to know if you have any lard he could use to soften up our Master's new saddle?"

"Of course, young Martin, here you go, regards to your dad, take this piece of cake for being so polite."

"Thank you very much."

"Any problem, son?"

"No, father, quite the opposite, I have seen a pretty young girl working for the cook a few times, I find her rather sweet with a sweet smile to match."

"And has this sweet thing noticed you, son?"

"We always smile at each other, Father."

"Tell your mum tonight you have found a sweetheart."

"Yes, ok, I will."

I told Mum, and Mum told Cook's sister, and she told Cook. A plan was hatched for us to meet casually one afternoon, when we were both given a few hours off, which is when we met.

"Meet anyone this afternoon, son?"

"Yes, father, as luck would have it, I met the sweet girl from the kitchen, Dora, although the cook calls her Nora."

"And?"

"Well, on the gallops this morning, the scent of the bluebells was overpowering, so I asked her if she would like a walk in the woods."

"And did she."

"Yes, so I kissed her cheek and after a few strides held her hand in mine."

"Then what?"

"I walked her back to the kitchen and kissed her other cheek and said, Oh, nothing."

"Hmmm?"

"Sorry, I said, may I see you again, She said yes, and I said, I think I am going to marry you."

"Well, well, wait till you tell mum that, how old is she, 14 going on fifteen."

"Come with me into the office, son, the time is perfect for me and you to have a chat about sensible young men and young ladies."

My father's advice, and as it turned out, the cook's advice to Dora, kept us on the right road. Not saying we never played or swam naked together, but we behaved like we should.

We courted for four years, and my Father asked the Master of the house for his permission for us to marry.

He said not only his permission but his blessing. He knew who we were, and he was grateful for our politeness whenever he saw us.

"Dora Hudson, would you do me the honour of becoming my wife? I have already sought the Master's permission through my father."

"Martin Allen Daniels, nothing would give me greater pleasure than to thank you for asking me."

The Master and Mistress of the house had made an old straw shed above the stables available for us to make it fit and livable. She even donated an old table and chairs, an old settee and some old wardrobes we could use.

Everyone at the big house did their bit to help us.

The house handyman made it windproof and installed two windows and a door for us.

My father made partitions to create a separate kitchen and bedroom, along with an ample space for another bedroom, should we ever need it.

We were married in the stable block, as tradition dictates, in 1913, and everyone attended, meaning everyone.

Cook baked and iced a cake for us, and the Master and Mistress provided all the food and drinks.

I could play the guitar, a footman played the squeeze box, a farm hand could drum, and my mum and Dora sang, and we all danced into the night.

On leaving, the Master and Mistress said how much they had loved it, and everyone could have an extra hour in bed in the morning.

The handyman offered three cheers for them, and we all obliged.

We went up the stairs for the first time as man and wife and into the marital bed. In the morning, we both agreed it was well worth the wait we had before finally having lovemaking.

I know your mum sees it much the same way as I do, son.

I am Dora, and when I was 12, my mother took me to Hareclough House for a job. Cook told my mum I was too young and skinny and to come back in a year.

Exactly on my 13th birthday, mum took me back to see the cook and went home without me. I was heartbroken and scolded by the cook for what would happen to me if I did not pull my socks up.

I dare not tell her I did not even own a pair of socks.

A maid took me upstairs, bathed me, and scrubbed my skin with a stiff brush to ensure I was clean and could not spread any germs.

"Not sure we have anything in your size, you skinny waif, if I told cook you were so skinny you would soon be over her table with her strap for company."

"Please don`t tell her, I beg you."

"See if you can find something in the outgrown basket."

"These pants and this vest should fit."

They did, and I found a dress which nearly fit, and I went back down to see the cook.

"Right, you do not look half bad in that uniform, and you have the sweetest face, go with Mary."

"You can help to set the table for the Master of the house and his wife. You may never see either of them. I have been here three years and haven't."

"Done that, cook, may I have another job?"

"Peel those potatoes and do not leave so much as an eye in them, or else."

I also peeled some carrots and cooked them until they were tender.

"Mop all the floors. What`s your name again?"

"Dora"

"Right, Nora, wash and dry everything dirty and put them on the table.

When that is done, you can sleep by the side of the fire and keep it lit.

If it goes out, so do you, out of the door onto the streets."

I did everything I was told, and when the cook came down from her bed.

"Good girl, Nora, you have done well, now go get yourself washed up in that sink."

It was easier to become Nora than say anything, so Nora I became.

After a week, I had accumulated one whole pound and had to give it to my mum when she called; it was no problem, as I had nothing to buy.

After six months, I had well established myself in my work and found my place.

Cook liked me, and I liked her a lot, and we chatted a lot.

She would sometimes save me the meat off the plates upstairs that they did not eat.

I was sent into town on errands for her or her sister, who was the house seamstress, and sometimes given a penny to spend, which I could use to buy some sweets.

"It's a bit quiet whilst the Master is away, Nora, you may go play by the stream, bear in mind, if you swim it`s in your vest and pants and not your dress, and definitely not naked like some of the older staff."

"I will cook, thank you for the time off and your advice."

I had seen a stable boy a few times when he was sent over by the stable head lad for something or another from the cook, and I hoped I would see him this afternoon.

"Hello, my name is Dora, but they all call me Nora, do I call you Sir?"

"Hello back to you, I have seen you a few times when I come in to see the cook for stuff. I am not a Sir, I am Martin, and I am 15. How old are you?"

"I am 14, Martin; please, will you be my friend?"

"Yes, of course I will, would you like me to call you Nora or Dora?"

"Nora, please, I do not want to upset the cook."

"Has she had to punish you yet?"

"Never had a need, and I suppose if she wanted, she would have."

"Nora, my dear, I will be your friend for life and will probably marry you."

"Oh, wow, Martin, I have never been married before."

He kissed my cheek.

"Would you like to walk through the woods with me? The scent of the Bluebells is intoxicating?"

"Yes, please, I would like that very much."

As we walked, he held my hand, and he made me the happiest girl in the world.

"Would you like to sit a while, Nora?"

"Yes, please."

He took off his jacket and laid it on the grass, and held my hand so I could sit gracefully.

We sat for about half an hour, and Martin showed me different birds and the names of some plants around us.

"Shall we go back so we are not late back, Nora?"

"Yes, please, Martin."

Again, he held my hand as he helped me up, and then walked me back to the kitchen, kissing my cheek again.

"Did you enjoy your free time, Nora? Did you swim?"

"No cook, may I ask a question?"

"Of course."

"Well, cook, I bumped into the boy from the stables who comes in sometimes to see you."

"That`ll be young Martin."

"Yes, it is, Martin, well, he asked me if I wished to walk with him through Bluebell wood."

"What did you think of that, Nora?"

"I thought it a better option than swimming cook, maybe that is not right, I dreamed I would see him."

"Anything else?"

"We sat, and he put his jacket on the floor and held my hand and helped me sit down, almost like a lady."

"Then what?"

"He pointed out different bids and plants and said he must get me back in good time, then I will not be scolded."

"Sounds like a gentleman, like his father is."

"He walked me to our kitchen door and kissed my cheek."

"Nothing else."

"No cook, nothing else, is all that allowed?"

"Of course, it is allowed, sweet child, and after you finish your chores tonight, come to my room. We need a little girl-to-girl chat."

Everything she told me I did or did not do as she advised, and in 1913, I became Mrs Martin

Alan Daniels, and we were given a room of our own to share above the stable.

"They were happy times, weren`t they, Dora?"

"Yes, they were. I could not think of anything to make it better in the years since we met. Those odd few hours we had off a week to actually be together as man and wife."

I confided in her then and even now, everything to cook; she had been like a second mum to me.

"You feeling ok, Nora, you look a bit peaky."

"Yes, thank you, well, if anything, a little tired."

"Everything working alright below?"

"Well, to be honest, I did not......."

"Say no more, my sweet girl, I think I know why you are with child."

We both cried, and I cried when I told Martin.

In 1916, we were blessed with a son, and Martin asked the Master if we could use his forename as our new son`s name. We got his blessing and a monetary gift for him, so Edward Martin Daniels was named.

"We are so lucky to have such a happy, contented son."

"As I am sure you were, too, love."

The master of the house received a daily paper, which was handed down to his butler, who then passed it on to Martin, ensuring he always had at least a day-old paper.

I then got it to read the women`s pages on all topics, from babies to food recipes to needlecraft. I usually finish off the crossword too, already attempted with two different coloured pens.

"What is the latest news, love?"

"Lots of chat about a war, Dora. I should sign up I will speak to the Master."

"I agree if that is your thought, Martin.

"May I have a word, Sir?"

"Of course, Martin, come in."

"Thank you, Sir, I am thinking along the lines of joining the armed services to fight, if necessary, for King and Country."

"Anyone in particular?"

"No, Sir, I was hoping you might suggest one."

"Yes, I can join my regiment now, and you can work your way up the command ladder. The way I see it, 1917 may be the last year we are not at war."

"I will take you to enrol in the morning in my regiment."

"Thank you, Sir, I accept your kind offer."

"The Master suggested I join his regiment, Dora."

"That was kind of him, did he say when?"

"Tomorrow!"

"Will you be home afterwards?"

"I don`t know, perhaps we should say our goodbyes today."

"How about right now, my darling?"

I was allowed to travel with the Master, and we went straight to the Company Headquarters.

He was obviously well up the ranks, as everyone in camp saluted him.

I just followed, and we were shown into an office.

"Welcome back, General. I see you, too, are seeing the probable outcome of this sorry affair?"

"Yes, Major, I felt it was time I took up rank again."

"And this chappie with you?"

"This is my stable Head Lad, he deals with all the outside staff and bookwork and feels he would be ideal at my side, easily Lieutenant material, and more.

He will sign up today, right, Martin?"

"Yes, Sir, quite correct."

I had signed up, and we were soon on our way home.

"Thank the Lord you have come back to us. Edward was wondering where his daddy was."

"All went well, and would you believe the Master is a General and he has asked that I be with him at all times."

"That comforts me, Martin, you will be side by side with a good, honest man."

"That I will, I have tomorrow at home then to train Dora."

My leaving day came all too soon. I said goodbye to my parents, then to my darlings, Dora and Edward, and set off in the carriage with The General.

So, I was left alone, the first time. The Master had told Martin he writes home every week or so, so he could too and share his envelope.

When I was having Edward, the cook had asked upstairs if there was any room in the Staff nursery for my baby.

She was told there was, and now they had four children under 4 years old, so apart from helping with the children, I could also be used as a maid.

Cook explained everything to me; it was not a problem, and I did not mind any work. I would do anything at all for the Mistress. They had always been good to me and Martin.

Martin was right in deducting from the newspapers that there would be a war, and we were aware of it from today. Cook had heard it on the house Butler's radio.

The day after the Master came home with Martin, both were in full uniform.

They both looked so handsome.

"Hello, my darling, how are you?"

"Apart from pinning for my brave husband, and Edward is well, how long have we got you for?"

"Just overnight, I was a private, made a corporal and now a Captain in charge of hundreds of men.

We sail out tomorrow afternoon, so I'm not sure where to or when I will be home."

I had a relatively easy birth with our second son, and I wrote to tell Martin, and I'm waiting for his reply with the boy's name.

"I do not mind as long as you come home, to me, Edward and my new baby bump."

The war went on for years, and I wrote and sent letters every couple of weeks. The Mistress allowed me to include my letter to Martin with hers for the General.

It finally happened, and the war was over, and the Master and my husband were on their way home.

I was told that he would be here in the afternoon, and I was given the afternoon off to get Edward his new son, whom he had never seen, Paul and me ready.

The staff we had left put up trimmings and buntings, and the ones who could play an instrument had practised for months to be able to play when they arrived and into the night.

We were also to have food, and a pig was put on the spit. I had helped cook and get her stuff ready.

What a night for us all! Not only did the General arrive home, but with him, Captain Martin Alan Daniels, we were no longer servants but almost middle-class.

Not that it would dramatically change our lives, we were happy with our lot.

In the coming months, our days and nights were lovingly spent.

Life was easier financially because Martin received an allowance from the government, given his position as a Captain.

The Master sent for Martin.

"Come in, Martin, I hope you are coming to terms with our calmer life now."

"Yes, but not easy, is it, Sir?"

"God no, I agree with you as I have for the past 4 or 5 years.

I have a proposition for you, Martin.

You saved my life on a few occasions during the war, and I would like to express my appreciation to you.

How would you like to become my gamekeeper for the whole estate?"

"Well, I know very little about gamekeeping, Sir."

"And what did you know about soldiering when I took you to camp?"

"I would be honoured to become your gamekeeper, Sir."

"Good, you will take over from Brooks, who has asked to be replaced now that he has reached 80 years old.

You will take over the gamekeeper's cottage and run my estate.

That pretty lass of yours could be your bookkeeper for the estate.

We will pay the pair of you £300 per annum, plus we will give you £50 to buy new furniture, what do you say to that?"

"Yes, Sir and thank you very much for your generosity."

"My life was worth heaps more than that Martin and I am forever indebted."

I did not tell Dora of my deed in saving the Master; it's men's talk.

We spent a month getting everything ready and moving in.

"I know I will bookkeep for you, Martin, but may I still keep some of my hours at the house?"

"Yes, of course, you do not want to lose track of the gossip and chit chat, do you?"

"No, I do not."

Hahahaha

The old gamekeeper took his dog with him, as working dogs and their owners often pair for life. So, I will buy a couple of Chocolate Labradors and start a new breeding line with Hareclough Hounds or Hareclough House in the name.

After a few months, we had our first litter of puppies. The mother and father had the same grandfather, so their names both started with "General," and thus my puppies would carry the name General Hareclough Peggy.

I always wanted a dog called Peggy, so I added it to my registered breeding name.

We soon had kennels full of dogs, and when we were on the Masters shoots, the gunners were impressed; as a result, the business of breeding and selling working Labradors began.

"I soon worked out by breeding two chocolate brown dogs, your % of brown to black was much higher. That said, many people liked the black colour of the breed.

I was settled into my new life as a loving wife and the mother of two wonderful boys, Edward and Paul.

Little did Martin Daniels realize what the world had in store for Captain Martin Alan Daniels.

Hareclough Heights

Chapter 3

SIBLINGS

Edward and Paul Daniels relished the life they had been born into; they had the best of all worlds at their feet.

They lived in a beautiful house with rooms they didn't even need or use; it was so spacious.

Always had puppies to play with, as well as playing with the children of the House and farm workers.

They were taught their school lessons in the big house with the Master's family, accompanied by a private teacher.

The beauty of Edward and Paul's birthright is that they did not know poverty and had nothing at all, yet they treated all as equals, and by the same token, were treated as equals.

The House school teacher comes in 5 mornings a week from 9 to 1

"Excuse me, Miss Rodgers."

"Yes, Edward dear?"

"Please may I ask some advice?"

"Anytime at all, Edward, please sit down. How can I help you?"

"As you know, Paul and I play with less fortunate children after school, not because we have to but because we want to."

"Yes, I notice, but young boys and girls are exactly that, Edward, young boys and girls who love to play out. As I have seen, the only difference among you all is that when you go swimming, you and Paul wear a pair of trunks."

"Well, Miss Rodgers, some of the children are keen also to learn, and I go through things with them. Am I doing wrong?"

"My word, no Edward, not at all, you are to be commended on your commitment to your fellow friends. Would you like me to help you set it up?"

"Wow, Miss Rodgers, yes please, my parents said, if it was alright with you, with it being almost winter, we could use our old home above the stables."

"Oh, yes, I agree and have a suggestion if you want it?"

"I sure would, Miss Rodgers, thank you for your kind offer."

"Why do you sit on separate chairs and tables when I teach you?"

"So we do not copy Miss Rodgers."

"Exactly, so with your students, sit them next to each other, so that they can copy and learn, rather than not learn. You look puzzled."

"Yes, Miss."

"Ok, you set them a puzzle, add together and write down, 2 + 2 = The ones who know it will put 4, the ones who do not know it will copy, and then they will know it too."

"Thank you, Miss Rodgers, for your invaluable advice."

I told mum, dad, and Paul at teatime, and they all said they would help.

After my class with Miss Rodgers, I taught the ones who wanted to learn in my mum and dad`s old home above the stables. My

Dad helped me make the lounge into a classroom, with wood across straw bales as desks and straw bales as seats. It was as comfortable as I could get it.

"Are you ok with your brother, Paul, helping you in your class, Edward?"

"Yes, mum, whilst Paul, although very clever, would never want to do anything like this on his own, he loves to help and to be honest is invaluable to me and our `Pupils`."

My parents provide the slates and chalk the children need, as well as a prize for Student of the Week, such as an apple, which they never get a chance to eat at home, or a few sweets.

As you would expect, we have a different child each week who wins, and with me having 14 students from 3 to 15 years old, it works well.

In 2 weeks, all my class knew the 2 times table and the 3 times table. They could repeat it and write it on their slates.

The Master of the house asked Edward and Paul to pop in and see him when they had a chance.

"You wanted to see us, Sir?"

"Yes, I did, thank you both for finding the time."

"You are always very welcome, Sir. We love serving you and all at Hareclough House.

"Good lad, now I hear from Miss Rodgers all you both are doing to educate the house staff`s children for the past two or three years."

"Yes, Sir, we call it an honour and a privilege to be able to do it."

"Now, to business, next month a course starts at the teacher training college to obviously teach you how to become a teacher, would this interest you both?"

"For me, Sir, yes, without doubt, Paul?"

"With respect, Sir, I am more at home helping Dad run the estate and farms, Sir, so I would decline your splendid offer, Sir."

"Well said, both of you. I will enrol you, Edward; no need to apply for a bursary. I will pay all costs and also pay you a wage. How old are you both now?"

"I am 17, Sir."

"And I'm almost 16, Sir."

You will both be added to the house payroll. The youngest, Paul, will receive £5 a week for now, and Edward, being 2 years older, will receive £7 a week. Is that agreeable to you both?"

"Yes, Sir, very generous."

"Thank you, Sir."

"Paul, I will ask about putting you on a land management course. Would you want that?"

"Yes, Sir, very much so, thank you."

At teatime, we told mum and dad of our good fortune.

"So, with us two now working under the Hareclough House banner and mum helping in the big house and doing all the paperwork for the estate, it was just perfect, especially with Dad absolutely loving looking after the estate, liaising with the head lad, running the stable, and caring for the 15 horses.

What in the world could happen to alter this?"

It was soon time for me to leave for my course, and Paul took over the school teaching with Mum's help.

My first year at the teacher training college passed so quickly, and it was the end-of-year ball.

I had no thoughts whatsoever of going; it wasn't really my cup of tea, anyway, and there was no one to take.

In the week before the ball, we had lectures from a Professor who would teach us, and another class from another part of the college on how to run mixed sex classes.

As we all got seated, I was lucky enough to sit next to a pretty girl. To get our attention, the Professor banged the cane he was holding onto his desk, CRACK.

"This will be one of the tools of your trade. Do you understand?"

A chorus of "Yes, Sir."

"You need to get the attention, then respect of your class, most will be used to punishment, but not many to the cut of the cane.

In the first class, choose someone who looks as if he needs caning, and as soon as he talks, have him stretch over your desk, bottom facing the class, for six of the best.

He needs to scream the place down and thus warn the class that the next time anyone is over a second, it's on the bare. Keep your eyes and ears open for a girl, same principle, but only three lashes and not as hard."

Apart from his fascination with corporal punishment, we were very interested in his talks, and we all learnt something.

He hit his desk hard again, CRACK.

The pretty girl next to me grabbed my arm and buried her head into my shoulder.

Lecture over, and she was still clinging onto me.

"There, there, the nasty cane has disappeared with its nasty owner."

"I am so sorry, Sir."

"No worries, let me walk you down by the river for some fresh air, if you wish."

"I wish it very much, Sir."

"I am Edward Daniels, and you?"

"Pleased to meet you, Edward. I am Elsie Warner."

We walked arm in arm and chatted, then she screamed.

"Whatever is the matter, Elsie?"

"I think I have been stung by something on my cheek."

A bee or a wasp was flying away.

"Let me suck out the sting for you."

I sucked on her cheek and spat out, and sucked again and spat out.

"I got it, you will be in a little pain for a while, but I have something for that."

Tears were rolling down her cheeks; I put my finger under her chin and lifted it.

We were looking eye to eye, and I kissed her soft lips. I lingered a few seconds.

She then put her finger under my chin, lifted, and kissed me for longer.

"Would you care to come back to my room so I can bathe your sting?"

As we climbed the two staircases to my room, we loosened our clothing.

Once inside, we kissed for longer as we undressed each other and lay on my bed.

I think we both said together, "Please be gentle", and we were.

We lay there naked, cooing and rubbing each other's arms and stuff.

She broke the silence.

"Edward?"

"Yes, Elsie?"

"May I have a go on top?"

Elsie and I spent the rest of the afternoon, that evening, and the Saturday morning after; I won't go on.

"What course are you on, Elsie?"

"The same as you, I guess, Edward, the first year of a year teacher training course."

"Yes, correct."

"Would you like to come and see my room, Edward?"

"Yes, please."

Elsie was stopping in a room identical to mine, right opposite.

We christened her bed as we did mine.

We were with each other as much as possible, morning, noon, and especially at night.

"It is the ball tomorrow evening, would you care to be my partner or...?"

She chose, or!

"Elsie, would you like to come and meet my family?"

"If you will come to meet mine first?"

"Yes, of course."

Her father was a farm manager on land adjoining the land that Dad and Paul look after.

"Edward, may I introduce my father, James, mum, Eliza, and younger sister Jill Towler?"

"Very pleased to meet you all."

"Where are you from, Edward?"

"My father is the estate manager for the General at Hareclough House, Sir."

"So, your father is Captain Martin Daniels?"

"Yes, Sir, you know him?"

"That I do, I served under them both in the last war, your dad is the bravest man I know."

"Thank you, Sir, erm, Sir?"

"Yes, son."

I cleared my throat.

"Please may I have the hand in marriage of your daughter, Elsie. I will honour love and protect her whilst ever I still draw breath?"

"Best ask the girl before I answer Edward."

I knelt on one knee.

"My darling Elsie, would you please do me the honour of becoming my wife?"

"Yes, I will, my dearest Edward."

Her mum passed me her wedding band, and I slipped it on Elsie`s finger.

"And it`s aye from me too, lad, get the port out, mother."

We all drank to the newly engaged couple, to me, and Elsie.

It is time we met my parents.

"Dad, Mum, Paul, Peggy, this is Elsie Towler. I have met her father and asked for her hand in marriage, and he said yes. I then proposed to Elsie, and she said yes."

"Would I be right in assuming your father is James Towler?"

"Yes, Sir, he is."

"A fine man and a brave soldier, you both have our blessing, right, Dora?"

"Yes, how wonderful, excuse me a moment."

"Edward, this was your grandma's engagement ring, if you would like it for your Elsie?"

"Elsie, please come over here."

I knelt and proposed again, and when she accepted, I slipped the ring on her finger, a perfect fit.

Mum and Elsie wept.

"I will make some tea."

"Please may I help you?"

"Of course, thank you, Elsie."

"Now, son, I must have a word."

"If I may interrupt, Sir, all the university rooms have contraceptives in the bedroom drawers."

"Excellent son, I am so proud of you and Paul, two wonderful sons."

When we left, we went to the big house to see the Master.

"Good evening, Sir, may I introduce my fiancé, Elsie Towler?"

"Any relation to James Towler, Elsie?"

"Yes, Sir, my father."

"Welcome to the family, young Elsie. You have chosen a good man."

"I know, Sir, thank you."

He shook my hand and kissed Elsie on the cheek.

Elsie and I went back to the uni to pack, as it was the end of the first year's term.

We spoke to the college room allocator and explained we were engaged and asked if it would be possible for us to have permission to share a room.

He showed us a lovely room on the ground floor with a magical view of the river and hills;

it was larger than the one we had last year and featured a kitchen and a small lounge.

During the second year of tutoring, we stayed at my parents' house for the weekend.

"Where will you live when you marry Edward?"

"We have not thought that far in front, Dad."

"Mum suggested you could use your old bedroom as your new bedroom and take the two rooms we do not use as a lounge and kitchen, or whatever you wish.

You can also use the side door as your door and be completely self-contained."

"That is such a lovely thought, and thank you, I will put it to Elsie as it would be her domain."

"That is a nice thing to say, son, after all, a good marriage is based on a good, thoughtful friendship."

We both went back for our last year in college; we had some tutorials the same, but differed in the subjects we wanted to specialize in.

I was more into maths and English, while Elsie was more into Geography and home-related activities like cooking and needlework.

"Do you think it is possible we could paint and erect a maypole for the children, so Elsie and I can plan a party for May Day, and every May Day to come?"

"Absolutely, Edward, what a lovely idea, Paul and I will look for a stout tree, and I think I know just the one."

At the weekend, Dad showed me the tree they had felled, some 12 feet tall.

He and Paul had taken all the bark off, and Elsie and I painted it red and white stripes.

We bought the eight ribbons from a shop near our college for the eight dancers. We had let the children choose the ribbon colours they liked, and I fastened them to the top.

Dad and Paul had dug a hole to put it in and made it so it could be taken out in winter and stored, perfect.

"I was thinking of a date for our wedding, have you any time you particularly fancy Elsie?"

"We finish our college life in May, and I feel it would not be right to sleep together at home till we are married, in respect to both our parents. They do not know about now, or don`t wish to know."

"That is another reason I love you so, Elsie, your thoughts of others. Would you like to lie on our bed with me and think of us?"

"Yes, please, my darling, remove your clothes so they do not get creased. Like I am."

We asked our respective parents if they had a preferred time, and both said the quicker the better; there was no point in waiting.

"How about the first of June 1936, Elsie?"

My exact thoughts, my dear Edward."

"I will go and see the General and talk to him about our plans." "I shall come too, Edward; in case we have to gang up on him."

Hahahaha

"Good morning, Sir, and thank you for seeing us so soon."

"Not a problem, Edward, you are like family, how can I help you today?"

"A few things, Sir, mum and dad said we could take a few rooms at the gamekeeper's house if that is ok with you."

"Absolutely perfect, means I will always see you both, the next thing?"

"We wish to get married on 1st June this year, Sir, if that suits you?"

"Perfect, had you planned where it would be held?"

"No, Sir, we waited for your permission."

"Well, in early June, the hay barn will be almost empty. How about in there?"

"Really, Sir, that would be most wonderful."

"Yes, really, Elsie, you know I have taken to you, not only because of who you are but mainly because you make Edward so happy. I can see the love in both your eyes."

"Thank you, Sir, that was a kind thing to say."

"If I may, I would like to finance the whole day for as many people as you wish. Perhaps an afternoon service followed by a pig and lamb roast, and enough beer to swim in. Maybe if we agree, the town's musicians will, so we can sing and dance well into the night."

I looked at Elsie as her eyes filled with tears, and we spoke together.

"Perfect, Sir."

"Before it is all agreed, go and speak to your parents, Elsie, for their agreement; they may have other plans, if so, I will not be offended in any way."

"Yes, we will, Sir, thank you for your consideration."

Elsie's parents were more than happy and asked if they could provide the hog and lamb, which, when we put the General in, he happily agreed to.

Our college year was soon to come to an end, and we had both secured jobs in the town's school.

Elsie, her mum, my mum, and the Lady of the House sorted everything out for the wedding.

"Paul, would you do me the honour of being my best man at my wedding?"

"Yes. I would indeed, brother, thank you for asking me."

"Excellent, you may even fancy one of Elsie's bridesmaids, how do you like your women, skinny, big busted, fat?"

"I will know if ever I meet her, Edward."

We hugged like we used to when we were young boys, showing our love for each other.

It was time, the day, the hour, the wedding and me waiting in the hay barn for my, to be, lifelong partner and wife.

The musicians began to play the wedding march. Let me explain what I saw.

"The barndoors were open, and a ball of light flooded in.

Right in the middle of the light was the beautiful vision.

My Elsie, top to toe in white, and her sister, the chief bridesmaid, looked equally gorgeous, along with three flower girls who sprinkled.

Petals all the way to where I was standing, waiting.

Her mum pulled back her veil, and the radiance of her beauty shone through.

As she walked towards with her dad, I realized what a lucky guy I am.

We said our vows, and I kissed my bride, and there we were, being applauded as we stood on the wooden stage we were married on

Tradition has it that the bride and groom say a home-made poem or sing a song.

I elected to sing a well-known song. "Ladies and gentlemen, I wish to dedicate this song to my new wife."

The band played the introduction, I held Elsie`s hand and sang.

Elsie, if you were the only girl in the world, and I were the only boy

Nothing else would matter in the world today.

I would go on loving you in the same old way.

Elsie`s turn, "Ladies and gentlemen, I wish to dedicate my poem to my new husband, Edward.

In a place not really far from me,

But a place which I could easily see

There lived a boy who is now a man.

Who smiled, only he can

I loved him then and still love him too.

And for that man, I said, I do.

Again, generous applause from our friends and loved ones.

I noticed the General's wife wiped away a tear of emotion.

Food was ready, and I think everyone had their fill.

Elsie's dad said he would leave all the meat for everyone to use for the next week or so, which was very generous of him.

Then the party got into full swing and moved outside under a bright moon and star-lit night, and even had the adults going around the maypole.

A great and brilliant day came to a close at 11:00.

The General once again declared that everyone could start 1 hour later in the morning.

Three cheers for the bride and groom and the Genera.

Hip Hip = Hooray

Hip Hip = Hooray

Hip Hip = Hooray

"Would you allow me to carry you over the threshold, Mrs Daniels?"

"Are your intentions towards me strictly honourable, Sir?"

"I am very doubtful on that question, I am afraid, Madam."

"In that case, I would not have it any other way, Mr Daniels."

We made love in the kitchen, lounge, and stairs before even reaching our bedroom door.

"Good to see you are a man of your word, Mr Daniels."

Chapter 4

WAR YEARS

We settled into married life, and both enjoyed our school jobs.

Education was growing in all areas, so it was time for school for all.

"How's your college going, Paul?"

"This sounds daft, but I am learning things I never knew possible to learn and have always taken for granted."

"Like what?"

"Well, working out acreage, so instead of saying, put them in the top field next to the wooden barn, we can say, put them in the 5 acres.

Or now we know the acreage works out the optimum cows per acre grazing, which is obviously a different amount to sheep."

"It sounds great, Paul and we can tell you consume all that knowledge with ease, don`t we, Elsie?"

"Yes, Edward, it shows on your face, Paul, you were almost dribbling as you spoke."

"What`s the dog situation like?"

"Incredible, Dad seems to have this special way with dogs, as if he talks to them and they understand and remember. Because of this, we have a waiting list and the bitches cannot spit the babies out quick enough."

"Is it just people in England buying them, Paul?"

"No, Elsie, all over the world, last week, four brown and three black labs were sent to Australia, by plane."

"Wow, they have travelled more than we have."

"Would you like one, Elsie?"

"Am I allowed, Edward?"

"I do not see why not. Could we be added to the list, please, Paul, but it will be a pet, so no need for Dad to train."

"Dog or a bitch, Elsie?"

"We do not mind, but we will call it Peggy."

Hahahaha

"Many children in the school now, Paul?"

"Just seven, and they are not old enough for infants yet."

"Are they learning, Paul?"

"It is more of a learning discipline, so they are not in bother when they are five and join the infant school. They are so keen to learn, most now their tables up to five and all can recite the Alphabet, forwards and backwards, so still worthwhile."

"Yes, for sure, I have an idea, why don't we move them out and fit it all out as it used to be for you to live in?"

"A sound idea, but why ever would I want to live on my own, do my own washing, make my own meals, should I go on, Edward?"

"No, point taken and well made."

"Must go, got some planning to do, bye for now."

"How nice to be able to chat with your brother Edward."

"Yes, very, all that talk of breeding and puppies has made me quite..."

"Yes, I see, follow me. Perhaps I may have a cure, but you will need to have it regularly."

"Sounds like just the tonic I need."

Our life was perfect, married to the girl I love, doing the jobs we both love and living in the same house with those I love. I really cannot see how life would get better.

I drew some plans, and my dad gave me some wood from his woodshed. With his help, I built Peggy an outside home and a run to be put in when we are both out at work or away somewhere else for the day.

Some say Labradors are only second to a beaver in the way they can and do chew wood and anything else, for that matter, given a chance.

I know what happens to dads inside dogs if they chew anything; let`s not go there.

When we get our little Peggy, she will be the best dog in the world, as long as she doesn't tend to chew excessively, I hope.

We were now two years into our teaching jobs, and I could sense that Elsie wanted to start a family. Could 1938 be the time we begin a new generation in the Daniels clan?

A message from the house came from the Master for Martin to go to his office.

"Hello Martin, thank you for coming so quickly."

"Never a problem for you, Sir."

"General!"

"Just as I thought, General, Sir, when are we needed?"

"We report to the camp next Monday. May I make a suggestion, Captain?"

"Please do, Sir."

"We should take young Edward with us to enrol, as you did, to obtain some position in the company."

"And Paul, Sir."

"With your consent, I have applied for him to have an exemption at present to run the estate."

"Yes, Sir, he is a proud lad, may I say you have asked if he would stay behind to run the estate for you?"

"Exactly that, thank you."

"No, Sir, thank you."

"What did the Master want Martin?"

"You mean, the General?"

"Just as you feared, my love."

"True, I have been expecting it a while, but hoped and prayed it would never happen. After the last war, the cost in human suffering was estimated as over 23 million dead and 17 million wounded in ways you could not imagine."

"I know, dear. Were Edward and Paul mentioned?"

"Let's talk about it at teatime, ask Edward and Elsie to join us, please."

We all gathered in our lounge, and Martin stood up.

"My dear family, I have some bad news, news most of us expected.

The war office has put us on a War Standing Position, meaning war is not probable, but imminent."

"I saw all the paper talk and felt it was Dad."

"The General called me in to see him today and told me the official situation. Paul asks if you, for the moment, will stay here and look after the whole estate, including the big house. It is my thinking too.

"I have to say I am not a fighting man but would do whatever you suggested, Dad, so yes, I accept the role."

Elsie was crying; she knew what was coming next.

"Edward, you have two choices. One wait for your enrolment, later this year or even next year."

"Or Sir?"

"Or come with the General and me and join up now, get some experience so you can progress up the command ladder."

"No need for discussion, Sir, I will fight for my country and my King, George V1."

"We leave home next Monday morning. We will be allowed limited leave leading up to our deployment."

"I will be beside you, Sir."

We all had a pretty silent tea.

"Come on, Elsie, we still need to work for the sake of our classes, and it will give me time to sort things with the head."

"I can take some of your classes, Edward, using your well-prepared notes from the past couple of years."

"Thank you, my love."

A few other teachers were doing the same as I was, and with Elsie's help, they could manage the increasing class size of 45 children in the short term, provided the war did not last for a couple of years, who knew?

Elsie and I had the weekend together; we were more passionate than ever, and it meant so much more somehow.

Monday morning, and I was packed and ready to go.

"Edward Daniels, do you promise to come home to me after the war, safe and sound?"

Elsie Daniels, I do so promise, and with the Captain and General looking after me, you can guarantee I will.

Mum, Elsie and the Lady of the house all waved us off, and I saw them crying and cuddling each other.

I think we three had eyes full of tears and hearts in turmoil.

Paul, I, and Elsie ate all our meals together and listened to the radio for news.

Here is an announcement from Nevill Chamberlain. He said what we dreaded

Today, September 3, 1939, it is with regret that I must inform you that we are at war.

He said they had failed to prevent conflict, so Britain and France declared war on Germany following the German invasion of Poland.

I turned the radio off, and as Elsie and I cried, Paul cuddled us and tried to give us some comfort.

Elsie had been distraught since Edward kissed her goodbye when he had a couple of days' leave, so I saw it as my job to try to lift her spirits.

I dare not tell her I never saw Martin for around 4 years during the last world war.

"Do not let slip you visiting your mum and dad every weekend or so, Elsie."

"I won`t, mum, I promise. I miss Edward so much."

"I know love, remember I have two to fret about in Martin and Edward, three with the General."

"Yes, of course, sorry mum."

We hugged each other as we cried. I was also emotional about the way she called me mum.

1941 Today`s news sees Germany now bombing England as well as bombing some of the countries in Europe.

Elsie, like I did, received at least one letter a month; the letters were placed with the generals, who received preferential treatment, their rank deserved.

I helped Elsie when we were not working to paint their part of the house to her own taste, not that in wartime we had a great choice.

The weeks and months soon turned into years.

1941 Today`s war news shows Germany expanding its war into Yugoslavia and Russia.

I could tell she was going downhill in health with missing Edward, but I had an idea to reverse this growing decline.

After tea, I began to teach Elsie some needlecraft; she was a natural, so that was the first part of my plan.

Elsie went to bed, and I spoke to Paul about the second part.

We all had breakfast, and Paul went out to work as we cleared the table and put everything away.

"Elsie, I can hear noises coming from your back door, maybe a squirrel or something."

"Thank you, dear Paul, will you come with me, please, mum?"

"Yes, of course, lead on."

The noise was coming from the dog run, and Elsie found a note on the fence of the run.

"Please help me, I am a poor orphan looking for a home."

Elsie opened the dog run and a chocolate brown bundle of a head, tail and legs, all over the place. She was so excited that she peed as she ran towards her.

She picked her up and cuddled her.

"Wait till I tell your daddy about you, Peggy."

"Ahh, you remembered the Peggy name, well done, Elsie."

"She is gorgeous, mum, thank you so much."

"Don`t thank me, thank Paul."

"Yeah, right, mum, this had nothing to do with you?"

I hugged Elsie and Peggy, and one of them nibbled my nose..

In 1942, as the war continued, the United States of America began sending troops to Britain.

Peggy was working, and as she got older, Elsie taught her more and more. She was obedient, as the breed is, and does as she is told, most of the time.

Sometimes things got chewed a little, after all, a coal shovel handle is easily confused with a juicy bone. And shoelaces do not get me started on shoelaces.

The most important thing is we now both laugh more than we cry, thank you, Peggy.

"Dear my darling Edward,

We both hope you, our dad, and the general are keeping quite well. I know you can never tell me where you are, even if you did know.

Darling, did you notice I said, `WE`?

I found a note on the kennel you made.

"Please help me, I am a poor orphan looking for a home."

She had found her way into the kennel. What do you make of that?

It was our very own Peggy.

As we have only owned her for two days, all I can tell you is she pees a lot, eats a lot, poops a lot and will lick your face all day.

I pray you will all keep safe, love Elsie, woof-woof Peggy xxx

When the time arrived to say farewell

I knew in my heart you would fare well

With all my love, I send to you

All you need to pull you through.

"What is so funny, son?"

"Elsie has started a family without me."

"How so?"

"Paul gave her a puppy."

"Ah, yes."

"You knew, ah, I see, mum working her magic, please thank her for me, dad."

My dearest darling Elsie and darling Peggy.

Thank you for your very welcome letter. I miss you so much it hurts.

Yes, we are all doing well and are kept very busy with war things.

Now what a clever puppy you have found us; she writes as well as picking a lock into the kennel.

Guard her with your life.

Much love from your devoted husband. XX

As we moved into the second and then third year of the war, and missing everyone so much, we just had to keep busy with other interests.

We help the staff decorate the House for Christmas and also assist in putting everything back into storage.

The same at Easter and Halloween.

1943, and important news from the war front, Russia has driven Germany further out of its country.

Elsie took some colour magazines to work for her class and to Paul's class.

Carefully, using scissors, the children cut out different parts of a page to stick on paper and create their own pictures and stories.

"Dear my darling Edward, and daddy.

We both hope you, our dad, and the general are keeping quite well.

Peggy has found herself pregnant, no soft way of putting it, my darling.

She was playing out quite nicely with a handsome chocolate Labrador from the kennels next door. I turned my back for two minutes, well, you know firsthand, my darling, what can happen to a girl who turns her back for two minutes!!!

I thought to myself, Hmm, Miss Peggy, you appear to be putting on weight.

Perhaps I should ask Uncle Paul to review her and provide his valuable insights on how we should proceed.

Doctor Whiston extends his very best regards and gratitude to you all and wishes you a safe passage in the future.

We love you with all our hearts, my darling Edward and Daddy. XX

For you, the time goes by so slowly

For me, the thought that you will know

I wish you to look after yourself

So you will keep in perfect health.

"What are you giggling about, Son?"

"Just two people deeply in love sort of chat, Dad."

In 1944, the English-speaking Americans landed on the beaches of France and liberated them from their German captors.

"What was that, mum?"

"Nothing much, love."

"Oh, ok."

"Sorry, love, I did not mean to snap. We have Christmas upon us next month, which will mark the war's impact on us, having taken away Christmases in 1939, 1940, 1941, 1942, and 1943, and soon to be 1944. However, I feel the end is very close, very close indeed.

1945 – Hot news, it is reported that Adolf Hitler has committed suicide on 30th April, as today, on the 7th of May, Germany signs an unconditional surrender.

"Elsie, Paul, come quickly."

"Whatever is the matter?"

"Germany has now surrendered, and everyone will be home soon."

"Can we ask the House if we can trim up the yard, maybe keep he maypole out and get the band in for a party?"

"Of course, sweet girl, I will go to see this afternoon after I have helped with needlecraft. Did you have a shiver, Elsie?"

"Yes, of excitement, mum."

"Good, I thought you might be coming down with something."

"Thank you again, mum, you are and have been a good mum and a great friend to me."

I went to help in the House, and the Lady came down.

"Have you heard the wonderful news, Dora? At last, after all the years and at a cost of millions and millions of lives, the Germans have surrendered?"

"Yes, Maa-am, I heard just before I came here. May I pass on a question from Elsie, please?"

"Why of course, I dare bet it is the same one I have come down for, please carry on, Dora."

"Can we have permission to trim........"

"Permission granted, that was exactly my thoughts too, I will get the workforce to get everything out we could need. I had also thought we could get the brass band to lead them all home from the station, and the soldiers could drop off as they pass their homes and bring everyone to a celebration here."

"Thank you, Ma'am. Elsie will be delighted."

"Ask Elsie to pop up and see me so that we can mix up our ideas."

"Will do, Ma'am, tomorrow about 10, alright."

"Just perfect, Dora, thank you. I will send the General letter this evening if you two have one to enclose."

"I was Elsie's day to work in our House school tomorrow, so I knew she would be free."

Elsie arrived for tea.

"How has your day been today, Elsie?"

"One of great excitement for the lucky ones whose daddies were coming home soon, I was then making banners."

"And the many poor daddy-less children?"

"To be honest, most did not really know him, so it was not as hard as you would think, so I had them start banners, My Daddy Was A Hero."

"So thoughtful, Elsie, well done,"

"Did you manage to pop up and see the Lady mum?"

"No, sorry."

Her smile faltered, and tears welled up in her eyes.

"She popped down to see me."

"Oh my goodness, what were her views?"

"She came down to say let`s trim up with bunting, flags, she had all sorts of ideas, so I told her you had too. She only asked if you would pop up tomorrow morning and share yours, 10.00, she said, I can cover class."

"She also said she is sending a letter tonight if we have one to enclose."

"Oh, how wonderful, mum, our men are coming home, and yes, I have a letter almost finished."

We both had a good cry, but happy tears.

"Whatever is the matter with you, too?"

"We are so happy, Paul, the war is done and all lucky enough to survive will be home soon."

"So, happy tears. Perfect."

"Elsie, love?"

"Yes, Paul, did you know your Peggy was out again and in the paddock asleep with the General's old horse?"

"Oh no, I did not, I will scold her."

"Please don't, she knows no better and is safe and with a friend."

"I will get her now, sorry, Paul."

"Bring her in here, Elsie, let's make a fuss of her. Paul, you pick everything chewable off the floor."

Peggy bounded in as if she were King of the castle, on the settee, on the armchair, paws on the table.

"How's the training going, Elsie?"

"Oh, you know, Peggy has taught me to sit and beg."

Hahahahaha.

"You would think that by a seven-year-old plus, she would be grasping the odd command, like not to nibble Uncle Paul`s fingers."

As luck would have it, we were having the last of the leg of lamb for tea, with mash and veg.

As soon as she smelt the lamb, Elsie gave her a command.

"Peggy, please show how you can sit, like a good girl, for the bone of Grandma Dora."

And she never moved, or hardly chewed a damn thing, the spindles of the chair backs seemed fair game as she was sitting right next to them.

My dearest darling Edward and Daddy.

We have heard the good news of your imminent return.

Peggy cannot wait to see her daddy. I have told her all about you and your loving ways, if you know what I mean.

I am helping to organize your homecoming and won't say anymore; I want it all to be a surprise.

I have all sorts to tell you and show you!

We love you with all our hearts, my darling
Edward and Daddy. XX

We wished you and your men Godspeed

When you all went off to war

We all here knew you would succeed

And prayed for all you saw

Chapter 5

WELCOME HOME

The house ground decorations were coming on a pace, with all the people here putting their ideas forward.

Apart from the General, Captain and our Edward, we had eleven house employees with them.

Sadly, on the day before the German surrender, the only two were killed together by a bomb, we are told.

They would never be forgotten, and Elsie had suggested to the Lady of the house that we honour in some way, and she had come back with, as Arthur was a stable hand, we would know the stables by Arthur's stable, Arthur's for short.

Billy was only 24 and such a lovely boy who tended the lawns and gardens with his dad.

The Lady suggested the formal garden would be known as Billy's Garden.

This was all subject to the agreement of the loved ones left behind.

"Elsie, would you put the formal suggestions to the ones who need to know. If they suggest anything else, say yes, and we will agree. Can you get some carvings done, not in memory of, but simply, Arthur's Stables and Billy's Garden?"

"Yes, Ma'am, thank you."

"Oh, Elsie?"

"Just a thought, during our celebrations, make a toast by the main garden and stables to our two brave boys."

"Thank you, Ma'am, what a lovely thought."

Elsie filled me in on all she knew and made notes in the planner she had prepared.

The big hay barn where Elsie and Edward were married was all but empty, so Elsie designed the inside to have more than one drinks station.

She had them placed one on each wall, and not on the barn door wall.

When she was talking to the Lady of the House, she suggested they order the barrels of beer with a third more water than usual. They both agreed the men would also be drinking free beer for England as well as fighting for England.

The Lady of the House had instructed the estate woodmen to cut trees and brash to build a bonfire to be seen in Germany; she and they knew it was impossible, but they got her meaning.

The two spits were back out, and once again, Elsie's dad provided a hog and a lamb.

The roast potatoes were grown in the estate's fields, as were the wheat and corn, which were milled to make the bread for the evening.

The highlight should be the huge firework display planned with no bangs; both Elsie and the Lady were mindful that the returning soldiers had had their fill of bangs over the six years at war.

It had also been agreed that the children and adults, too, if they wished, could come in fancy dress.

Paul had organized numerous games and pony rides for the children in the afternoon, and Elsie had purchased many chocolate sweets as prizes. Chocolate, as most children had never tasted it in their lives.

"How are the welcome home plans going, Elsie?"

"Very, very well, hopefully the highlight of the day was to be a Dog show, pet dogs only, no working ones.

One of the estate workers made me a simple but appropriate trophy shaped like a bone."

"How many have entered so far. Elsie?"

"Just one stunning example. mum."

"Let me think who that could be."

"Please do not tax your brain, mum, the show is off."

"Oh no, why?"

"Mentioning no names, but someone took the trophy off the table."

"And?"

"And ate it, mum."

Hahahahaha

I dropped my cake mixing spoon, laughing, and when I bent to pick it up, it had disappeared.

"Mum, you know the small cuddly frog Edward bought me before they left?"

"Yes, the green one?"

"That's it, well, it keeps disappearing, and do you know where I find it?"

"Half eaten, I suspect."

"No, that is the odd thing, in her basket next to her. I ask her for it, and she puts it on my knee and snuggles up to me."

"Now that is bizarre!"

A knock on my door, not a woof from Elsie's guard dog.

"Hello, hello?"

"Hello, Ma'am, please come in."

"So sorry to interrupt, but urgent news."

"Thank you, Ma'am, please take a seat."

Peggy was still fast asleep.

"I take it I will be safe and not mauled?"

"It has to be at your own risk, Ma'am. Peggy is trained to, well, trained to, not trained at all, Ma'am, so does as she likes."

"My news is the soldiers' train will arrive on Saturday afternoon at 2.30, how good is that?"

The Lady began to weep. I knelt to console her and joined her in tears. Elsie joined us, and she is not a bit of good in a situation like this. We all wept and got ourselves together, except Elsie.

I went to see her out, and she leaned forward and kissed my cheek.

"Thank you for your brilliant support these past six years or so. I would have given up long ago had you not been there."

"You are very generous with your praise, Ma'am."

"I am now Elisabeth to you, Dora."

I kissed her cheek as she left.

"ELSIE"

"What,"

"Snap out of it, girl, you are going to wake Peggy up."

Hahahaha.

That must be the best news a service member's loved one could ever receive.

How are your plans progressing, "Elsie?"

"Really well, my dad has had the hog and lamb hanging for over 10 days, so that a few more days will be perfect. He said he would send a couple of his farmhands down to roast and serve it, then we can all enjoy the celebrations."

"You did invite your parents, Elsie?"

"I never thought to."

"How many farmhands does he have working for him?"

"Total, including their families under 20."

"Then invite the whole lot of them down with their war heroes or not to help us celebrate. I will clear it with Elisabeth."

"Ooww get you, Elizabeth!"

"Get out of here, you cheeky monkey, and take sleeping beauty with you."

"PEGGY."

And they were gone.

"Will everyone be ready for us when we get back, Dad? Oh, can I call you Dad, or should I still say Captain?"

The General looked at us both. After all we have been through together over the past six years, we are soon to be back in England. "I am now Edward to you two as you two are Martin and Edward, and both VCs at that, I am a very, very proud man. Cough, cough, cough."

"Thank you, Sir."

"By my reckoning, we should be reaching the channel in the morning, then home to our loved ones in the afternoon, please God."

"Cough, cough, cough."

"First job for you, Edward, is to get that cough sorted out."

"Yes, I agree, Martin, those wet squelchy trenches we were in did not help."

"Why were some officers in a field tent and not with the men in the trenches, Sir?"

"Because dear boy, they were the sensible ones, cough, cough, cough, and do not have an infernal cough. I appreciate the respect you are showing me, Edward, when I said I was Edward."

"It is how mum and dad brought us up, Sir. There are times I call my dad, Sir."

"As I recall, Edward, the times you knew you were in trouble, do you think?"

"I could not possibly comment, Dad."

"Do you know where they are, Mum?"

"All I can tell you is they will sail the English Channel late evening, early morning on Friday, to catch the train home.

The war office gives very little away even when not in war."

"How are your plans doing? Are you on schedule?"

"Yes, just the horse chestnuts to put in the oven in the morning, and I am done. I want to give Edward my 100% attention tomorrow."

"And rightly so, Elsie."

"Probably the same as you and Edward's mum, even though you are old."

Hahahaha

The hours on Friday seemed to be the length of a week.

Looking out of our bedroom window across the bright green fields to the river. My, how we used to swim in there, sometimes with costumes on and a lot of us, other times, more personal and skinny dipping, which means naked.

We would make love in the sandy area where we left our clothes. Then back into the wash to wash away the sand, and sometimes in a clinch we would......

Anyway, daydreaming does not get my baking for tomorrow done.

"Hello, hello, Dora."

"Coming, Elisabeth. Sorry, I was looking over the fields and daydreaming of our youth."

"Such happy days, Dora, I have spent many a day at our bedroom window imagining Edward was coming towards me, then I would carry those thoughts into my dreams.

Anyway, how is your baking doing?"

"Very well, last lot in now, and yours?"

"An absolute disaster, the cook has banned me from downstairs at present."

"We all have our specialties, don`t we?"

"Erm, not sure I have found mine as yet, dear."

"Cup of tea, Elisabeth?"

"That would be super, thank you."

We always use our milk jug, but we also got out our sugar basin, just in case.

Best cups and saucers, of course.

"Just a little milk for me, my dear."

"Would it be too adventurous to have a slice of my winter parkin with a little butter on, do you think?"

"If it is, it will be the most adventurous I have been in years, if not decades."

We sat and talked, and I poured us another cup of tea.

"I won't cry, but do you want to know my top regret is Dora, during and before the war?"

"Yes, if you are willing to share."

"It is not knowing you better. The times I have sat in our drawing room scrying, I was so lonely."

She did cry, and I moved closer to comfort her.

"Good to say that is all in the past now, Elisabeth, you are now my best friend."

"Oh, Dora."

Followed by more tears.

"Elisabeth, we are taking two open-top carriages to be at their homecoming on the station platform. Would you care to join us? You could come out with us and have the General all to yourself on your way back?"

"Oh Dora, I would adore to, thank you for asking and being my newest and most favourite friend."

"A jam tart, Elisabeth."

"Only if it obliges you, dear."

"Yes, it does, massively."

I cleared our plates.

"If you wash, I will dry your beautiful crockery."

"May I ask if you are an expert at it?"

"You may ask, already knowing the answer, Dora."

Hahahaha

As she left, I walked her to her door, admiring all the work being carried out and all but completed.

"Dora, not sure I have looked this pretty since Edward and Elsie's wedding."

"I do believe you are right."

I kissed her cheek and pulled her towards me, holding her for a few seconds. As we parted, we smiled at each other.

"Thank you so much for that gesture, Dora; it made me very happy."

She squeezed my hand as we separated.

I felt exhausted, so I went back up to our bedroom and had a nap.

I was awoken with a kiss, then another, then another. I opened my eyes, and Peggy snuggled into me.

"Hello, girl, how did you get here?"

"Are you up there, Mum?"

Woof

"She asked me, and not you, Peggy. Coming, Elsie."

"Sorry, were you asleep?"

"Yes, but it is ok, just trying to pass the hours quicker."

I told her about Elisabeth's visit; she was sad for the past few years, but happy that she opened up to me.

"At last, we are at the harbour for our boat."

"Us and about 100,000 others, Dad."

"At least we have births booked, Edward."

"That is coming home consolation, the hours it is taking on our way home seem 10 times longer than the hours on the front!"

"What are you expecting, chaps, a quiet reunion with our loved ones?"

"With mum and Elsie organizing Sir, I would suggest a quiet reunion with wives would mean us getting off the train at the station before ours."

Hahahaha

"I suppose so, Edward, and not such a bad idea for the men and our workforce, they could all do with a jolly good time."

"I have a new family member to get acquainted with, too, right, Dad?"

"Let`s hope you have some furniture to sit on, you know the saying, don`t you, Edward?"

"No, Sir, having a Labrador for a pet, regardless of colour, is like inviting a swarm of termites to live in."

"Oh dear. So glad I built an outside kennel."

"Made of fortified tank steel?"

"No, Sir, wood."

They both nearly fell off the pier laughing, and I joined in.

"May I show you the dining room, Sirs?"

"Have we births booked?"

"Sorry, Sir, no births on board. Calais to Dover will only take 2 hours, Sir."

"Ah, I see, thank you, lead on."

That is a blessing to me. I have found I am a poor sailor.

We had a drop of whisky and a coffee with cake, and we had docked.

We caught the train from Dover to London; I was fascinated by the English countryside.

Dad found a paper and was reading from cover to cover.

The poor General slept, snored and coughed.

We waited for about an hour for our train home.

When it arrived, we were shown into a first-class carriage with other officers.

We were served lunch, which included roast beef, Yorkshire puddings, roasted potatoes, and vegetables, along with any spirit or beer we wanted.

I couldn't believe we were on our way home after six whole years away.

After our meal, we were offered tea or coffee, and they left the pot for us to keep the General's cough lubricated.

As we got closer and closer to home, I began to recognize station names.

The next stop was ours.

We were told the next train in was the London one, and we were shown in which area of the platform the carriage we wanted would stop.

Elisabeth had organized two long trailers with sides, complete with barrels of beer, for the returning soldiers and their families.

We could see the plume of smoke in the sky getting closer and closer, and heard the train whistle as it went through the short tunnel.

There it was, at last, the sight of the train was all we needed, and although I had sworn I would not cry, I was the first one to blubber.

We held each other as the train door opened, and out they came. The General, Martin, and Edward, dressed in full dress, went onto the platform. Elisabeth could not wait, and we followed her, jumping into our own husbands' arms.

We were the last out of the station; the trailers were loaded with returning soldiers, their families, and the brass band that would lead us home, nearer Hareclough House.

Elisabeth and the General got into their carriage, and we four into ours, and we all set off.

We only had to travel about 2 miles, and our driver was instructed to stop a quarter of a mile out.

We stopped, and the brass band tuned up and looked at Elisabeth for a nod to start.

The sound was deafening, not only from the band but from the two trailers full of people who disembarked.

What a sight, emotional, spectacular, and well worth it for the brave men of the Second World War's homecoming.

The smell of he hogg and lamb roasts drifted on the light breeze.

We were happy to see our boys home alright.

Paul and a few of his friends took ALL the children to the river beach for swimming and games.

This left the soldiers and their wives to become reacquainted again, in privacy.

"Did you help organise today, Elsie?"

"I played my part, yes."

"Whatever happened to the kennel I built? It is in pieces."

"That must be the 10th kennel, Edward."

"Before I open the door, be prepared for the pack of dogs ascending on you. Our little girl does get overexcited."

As I opened the door, I shouted a command.

"Sit, Peggy."

We went in, and guess what, she was sitting.

"Someone has swapped us dogs, Edward. Come and see your daddy, Peggy, the one I have told you about all these years."

She ran towards him, so excited, as Edward was.

We all sat on the settee, and Peggy ran upstairs. I knew why; she was so clever.

She ran back downstairs, jumped onto the settee and put my froggy on Edward`s knee.

"She often goes up and gets it and sleeps with it in her basket."

"Because she is the most beautiful girl in the whole world."

"I have a surprise for you both."

I ran upstairs, then back into the kitchen.

"Look what Mummy has for Peggy. Now sit and take your bone, nicely."

I locked her in the kitchen.

"Now, my darling husband, your surprise."

We walked hand in hand upstairs to what was a small storeroom but was now a bathroom with a foaming bath just waiting for one or two people.

I washed Edward from head to toe, and he moaned at the attention he was getting. I then undressed and joined him, and I moaned with him.

Two hours later, the brass band struck up again, and the evening's activities began. All the posts with lit-up ends illuminated the whole area.

People ate, danced, played, or just ran around. The mood was so inspired.

The younger lovers, Elsie and Edward, included, would often smooch to the slower songs or kiss and cuddle in the adult area we had created, with reduced lighting and no children.

8.00 pm, and the brass band were stood down, and the cook had an area where they could secure their instruments.

The modern music band took over the barn, and the night began to swing.

The fire was lit at 9:00, and fireworks and rockets illuminated the sky, with not a single bang.

People began to drift away, the Master and his wife first; most had commented on his coughing and knew only too well what it could be.

The rear of the barn had been set aside with hay on the floor and blankets; this was for the

Brass Band and the other musical group to bed down in if they did not want to walk home.

Paul was to ensure all lit flames were out and left the flickering light as the bonfire burnt itself out.

All but two of our extended family were home, safe and well, but for some, the war would never be over. The battlefields were exchanged for the battles in their minds.

Shouts and screams echoed around the grounds when some of the old soldiers slept and dreamed.

God Save The King

Hareclough Heights

Chapter 6

ESTATE TOUR

I'm not sure who slept, who played, and who had nightmares, but I'm sure every single one was up at 8:00 am helping to tidy up.

The musicians were fed, the Brass Band took our trailer home, but the modern band stayed and played all the songs of the day.

"Hello Elisabeth, are you taking in this wonderful air?"

"No, Dora, if it's ok, I wish to help, and no light duties."

"You are more than welcome. Could you help carve the meat off the spits, please, and no pinching the crackling. That can go separately as treats for the school children.

"When did it become Elisabeth and Dora?"

"Far too late in the war, Martin, only a few months, she is a lovely lady, and we have become pretty close."

"How strange, the exact thing happened with us on our way home, the General said to call him Edward. He really is ill, Dora, and I am worried for him."

"I thought that in the trap on the way home, pneumonia, do you think?"

"Yes, I do, he had been bad with it 18 months or more."

"I have a question, my darling?"

"Yes, Martin, ask away."

"How come not one person was blind drunk last night with all that free ale about?"

"Very easy, Martin, our Elsie ordered the ale and asked for extra fresh water in the barrels."

"Genius."

So, the workers worked and sang as did Elisabeth.

The spit was dismantled, washed and put back in the shed it came from.

The two meats were carved and placed into two meat safes in the barn, allowing people to help themselves. The crackling was broken into small pieces and put into a cake tin to keep it crisp.

The children were poking the embers of the fire, watched by but not stopped by the older children. What is it with people, fires and sticks?

"Two o`clock and all done, thank you all very much indeed for your warm welcome to our courageous men and not forgetting the two brave men we lost.

They were buried where they fell, and so the Master has instructed me to tell you we will be building a monument to them to honour the most significant sacrifice of all, thank you."

"Three cheers for the Master and Mistress."

Hip Hip – Hooray

Hip Hip – Hooray

Hip Hip - Hooray

"Would you like a walk by the river, Edward?"

"Could that be a proposition, Elsie?"

"Quite easily, my love."

"Shall I go and get Peggy?"

"Perhaps not this time, she needs 500% watching."

"Shall we ask Edward and Elsie for tea, Martin?"

"Yes, that would be lovely, what are we having?"

"A choice tonight."

"I just love being spoilt?"

"You are worth it, darling."

"What is the choice?"

"Oh, lamb or pork."

Hahahahaha

"Edward, when do you think you will start work again?"

"Tomorrow I thought, everyone has done so well covering for me, I owe it to them to try and make it easier."

"Promise me one thing, darling."

"Of course, anything."

"Promise me you only work Monday, Wednesday and Friday for a month or so until you feel you are into it again."

"I promise, and a good idea, thank you. Let`s go for tea, yes, you too, Peggy Woo."

"You were late getting back from your walk, so I let Peggy out for a pee."

"Yes, sorry mum, something came up!"

"How are you feeling to be home, Dad?"

"To be honest, Elsie, I still feel I am still in travel, being shaken to bits, but I am so happy to be home with all those I love."

Woof

"Oh, and all those I am still getting to know. Does she always nibble people's fingers?"

"Yes, she does."

"And if she, ouch, does not like you?"

"Let us not go there."

Hahahahaha

Sunday is here, and it's time for church. I think we are all part of a local church somewhere.

There is not much difference between them, except that one is stricter.

Our Minister is Dr Spence. I think he must be over 100 years old, ok, a slight exaggeration, but I think he christened my grandma!

I have always helped out on Sundays, starting in Sunday school and then becoming a Sunday school teacher. Now I do the refreshments with others after our service.

God is very important to us, whether you have nothing at all or Millions. He is the same one, so our faith is non-discriminative; he has time for all.

Sometimes he does things you don't understand, but we find strength in him just being there.

"Are we all ready?"

Woof

"Not you just yet, Peggy. When we come back, go get froggy and go in your basket."

"As if she understands that."

"Just wait and see, Edward."

"Well, I`ll be..."

"Told you, are you three ready?"

We all set off in Martin's trap, him driving, if that's what it's called.

Martin said that the General was going to order a car for us all to use when we got back, and the second day he was back, he did so.

"Martin, what car did you say the Master ordered?"

"It is called a Humber Super Snipe, like we have at the army base. It is big and luxurious, and he said it fits his status, not sure if he meant it or if it was tongue in cheek."

"Probably both, Elisabeth would love that, especially if they have a chauffeur."

"Good morning, Dr Spence, it sure has been a long time since I have waited to say that."

"And a long time I have had praying for my flock to return, safe and well, do you do a manly hug, Martin?"

"Hug, I could almost kiss you."

They had a lovely hug, Edward too.

"May I ask a favour, Dr Spence?"

"Of course, Martin."

"When the General comes, could you give him one too, and thank him for bringing us back home?"

"Of course I will, it is the new thing the kids are doing, and I love it, Mrs Spence says I should and my age and not my shoe size!"

It was a beautiful welcome home service. The General coughed most of the way through it.

After the service, when we were shaking hands with our minister, the General took a slight tumble, to be honest, I think it was more of a feint.

Edward was there to catch him and help him back to his trap.

"Thank you, Edward, you have always been there for me these past few years, and I bless you for it.

We all went to Edward and Elsie's for a light lunch, consisting of a few cheeses and tomatoes, or egg and cress sandwiches, and some biscuits she had baked. Peggy did not know who to befriend first, but Martin ended up with her snuggled up and froggy on his knee.

"Shall we take Pegs for a walk, Edward?"

"Yes, somewhere I want to show you."

"Mysteries, I love mysteries."

We walked out and away from the main house to a small plot of land.

"What do you think of this area here, Elsie? It is my preferred place to build a home for us. Which would be your special place?"

"Why, right here with you, my darling."

Hahahaha

We both laughed.

"It was not meant to be the brilliant joke it turned out to be, Edward. I will rephrase it. I love this very spot, we can see the river and our sandy beach, and we can see and hear from the big house. Why do you ask?"

"When we were away, the General spoke of everything we had and wished we had.

"Think of home and those we love who are waiting for us, and now think where would your perfect house be, anywhere in the world?"

"I said on this very spot."

"A good choice, Edward. Now, when you close your eyes at night, plan it out."

"And instead of war dreams, I dreamt of you and me planning and building our own home."

"Perhaps one day, Edward, why don`t we save a little each week for it?"

"Our building fund for spare money, what a lovely idea, it will also help my dreams, Elsie."

We kissed and had a loving cuddle, yes, all three of us.

"Would you like to come for tea tonight, you two?"

"Yes, please, mum, let us bring the meat."

Hahahahaha

It was a lovely meal with all those we loved, including Peggy. Did we take it everywhere here, you may wonder. Yes, it was safer when she was in the chewing mode; nothing was safe.

When we got home, I ran us a bath; it was a relaxing time, as I had work the next morning and wanted to take Edward's mind off it.

We lay in bed and kissed goodnight.

"Think where we would put a steel kennel in our new house, Edward?"

"Will darling, sleep well."

We both sounded well, and when Edward woke.

"In the outbuilding, I built a Peggy Woo-proof kennel."

Love it when a plan comes together.

"What would you like for breakfast, Edward?"

"How long have we got?"

"About toast or nothing."

"Toast, I think love."

As we left home, Dr Howard was pulling up in his chauffeur-driven limousine. The door was opened for him, and he came over and shook my hand, so I gave him the man hug I had been taught this morning.

"Welcome home, son, and please give my very best regards to your father, oh.

"Yes, I will, Sir."

"That was my first man-to-man cuddle."

"It was a hug, Sir."

"A hug, you say, well, it was very welcome, may I use myself Edward?"

"But of course, Sir, but mainly for those you love or have been missed."

He walked towards the big house.

"Hm, hug you say."

At last, I was back at work with children willing to learn.

I walked into the classroom and all the pupils stood up and applauded me.

"Thank you, please sit down, I feel honoured by your generous applause.

I'd like to give you a brief test, not to grade you, but to assess your progress in your learning.

Please copy down the sums I write on the board, but do not answer any yet.

Now, of the ten questions listed, put a line through the ones you could answer.

Who crossed out 4? Good, all of you.

Anyone crossed out 6, just 2, perfect, we start at question 5.

"How did your day go, Edward?"

"Like a dream, but so tired."

"Not too tired, Edward?"

"Never too tired, my love, bath?"

"Delightful, my love."

The days I worked, I loved; the days I rested, I loved, and the lady I had at home, I loved.

Over the next few weeks, a live-in nurse was employed at the big house.

"Good afternoon, Elisabeth. I believe the General wished to see me."

"Yes, Martin, thank you for coming so promptly."

"How is he at present?"

"Best as I could say is, tolerable. He does not understand what is happening to him, and why."

I opened my arms and Elisabeth accepted my hugs. I will thank Dr Spence for the rest of my life for that part of his Christianity teaching.

I was shown into the bedroom, and he was sitting up in bed.

"Good morning, General, how can I help?

"It`s Edward, Martin, but call me what you are most comfortable with."

"Thank you, Sir."

"I just wanted an update on everything since we got back. I am stuck in here all day and see nothing."

"Well, Sir, how`s about you get dressed and take you for a tour round the estate in the single trap?"

"Really?"

"Yes, really, Sir.

"I do not see why not, for goodness's sake, it is not going to kill me, is it?"

"I would suggest not, Sir. I will get things ready, say, half an hour?"

"Perfect."

"He wants you, Elisabeth. I am going to take him around the estate."

She hugged me this time.

"Thank you so much, Martin. I am indebted to you."

"Hello Jeff, could you hook up Caper to the two traps, please? I am taking the General out."

"That is brilliant, Martin. I will put a few thick rugs in."

The General was still able to get about, and we walked him halfway up the horse mounting steps to make it easier for him to get in the trap.

It became a daily event, and into the second week, I knew I would be busy one day.

"Edward?"

"Yes, Dad."

"Could you do me a favour, please?"

"Yes, anything."

"Would you take the General out in the trap for an hour or so?"

"Would be honoured to, Dad, thanks for asking."

"Good morning, Sir. I will be your driver and guide for the day. I hope you do not mind?"

"Mind, it will be a delight, Edward."

I took him to various places, and we mostly talked about me, Elsie, and our daily work.

"So, you have adapted well back into civilian life?"

"Yes, Sir, Elsie has been the stable influence I needed."

"You are a good match, like me and my Elisabeth. I love her more and more each day, well, the days I have left."

"I will not say do not talk like that, Sir, as it is inevitable for us all, we will meet our maker. The same maker we prayed to as we fought around Europe."

"So true and such wise words from a young man, you have cheered me up no end, thank you."

"You are very generous with your words, Sir."

"Now, take me to the place I had you dreaming about, Edward."

"Mine and Elsie`s house site, Sir?"

"Yes, if you don`t mind, another question, if I may."

"Of course, Sir, anything."

"Why did you choose Caper instead of Jet to pull the trap?"

"Easy, Sir, I foaled her."

"That explains it, thank you."

"This is the spot, right here, Sir."

Elsie had been baking ginger biscuits, so I made a flask of tea and took some ginger with me.

"A cup of tea and a home-made ginger biscuit or two, Sir."

"Yes, if only."

"Well, it is only Sir."

I had taken 2 Chinese cups and poured us both a cup of tea, and spent many a minute dunking gingers in.

"A drop more, Sir?"

"Yes, please, Edward."

"Another ginger, Sir?"

He sipped and dipped.

"I see why you would choose this place, Edward, the river Tauper in all its mysterious glory. I wish I had a pound for all the times I skinny dipped off that sandy beach."

"Me, Elsie and too, Sir, and still do."

"What happens if you are seen, Edward?"

"When the hormones kick in, Sir, we could be in front of an audience and not see them."

"That`s my boy, talking of which, when will we see little Daniels about?"

"Well, we have a four-legged Daniels in Peggy Sir, have you met her?"

"No, but I would like to."

"Then our next stop, Sir, if you wish."

"Oh, I wish, alright, anything to keep me out of my bed, son."

"Would you like to keep up here or onto the ground, Sir?"

"Ground, I think, if that suits?"

I pulled Caper up by the steps and helped the General down, then sat him on a straw bale while I took the trap back.

I passed him his walking cane and helped him to our door.

"Peggy, Sit."

I opened the door, and she was sitting waiting for her next instruction.

"Stay."

I sat him on the settee and put the kettle on, it was Tuesday, I was not working, but Elsie was.

"Good girl, Peggy, this is the general, be gentle."

I went to make some tea, and Peggy flew up the stairs.

I sat next to the General.

"She obviously did not take to me."

"Not so hasty, Sir."

I heard her coming back down.

"Not so hasty, Sir."

Up she jumped onto the settee and placed Froggy onto the General's knee.

I explained to Froggy, and it brought a smile to his face as Peggy snuggled into him and he stroked her.

"Thank you for the tour and tea and introduction to Peggy, Edward, the best few hours I have spent for years and years."

"Is it home time, Sir?"

"Aye, I think it is my nap time."

We slowly walked back to the House; Peggy never left the General's side.

"Welcome home, Edward. I can call the search parties off now."

"So sorry, Ma'am."

"Elisabeth, please, and I was only joking, anything to report?"

I winked and pointed outside.

"If you are comfy, love, I will see Edward out."

"Yes, I am, thank you for sharing your dream, all you have done for me today, son."

"More than welcome, Sir."

"No, Edward, what is to report?"

"In something like 2 hours or more, the General only coughed 4 or 5 times, so the fresh air is doing him more than good,"

"That is wonderful news."

"I was thinking if we got him a wheelchair with big back wheels, he could manage himself, he could be wandering outdoors, watching and chatting."

"I will see to that at once. They named you well, Edward."

"Thank you, Ma-, I mean Elisabeth. Come on, Peggy."

We walked to the end of the lane to meet Elsie off the countryside bus from work, and told her about our day, and listened to hers.

"Please, can I run the worker of the day a nice bath, with all the trimmings?"

"Only sounds delicious, Edward, well worth hurrying home for."

Work went well again on Wednesday, my second day, and the whole class got their homework correct. I had set them; what a pleasure it was to teach them.

Luckily, I was off work on Thursday when the General's car came. It took me back to the Army camp, where all the top echelon had access to one, including the General.

It was not a new one, as we were still under rationing, even with cars, but it was immaculate, standing outside the House, all in black.

It still had the smell of new leather inside.

"Do you feel like a runout somewhere, General or a trip in the trap, Sir?"

"I think the trap today, Edward."

He was in his wheelchair, and I pushed him into the barn and left him till we got Caper hitched up.

He got up and sat in the same position as he had before.

We had an hour and chatted the whole time.

"Cup of tea plus extras, Sir?"

"That would be nice, thank you."

I poured our tea into identical China cups and offered him a biscuit with currants from Elsie's home bakery. He took one and dunked it.

Another biscuit or top up, Sir?"

"No, thank you very much. Do you mind if we head back now, Edward? I feel a little funny."

"Of course, Sir."

I got him into his wheelchair, and a lad took Caper and the trap back up to the stable.

The house butler was waiting.

"Welcome back, Sir. May I take you in?"

"Yes, just a moment, Edward?"

"Yes, Sir."

"Would you give me one of your hugs? You never know, it might be the last time."

Of course, Sir, and please do not say that."

He kissed my cheek, the first ever off a man, and went in, and I just wondered.

I went to see Dad at the kennels.

"Hello, son, can I help you?"

"I am worried, Sir?"

"Worried about what for heaven's sake?"

"The General, Sir, I am afraid I fear the worst."

I told him about the car, the trap and the hug.

"I will pop and see him about something now?"

"What?"

"I will make it up on my way."

"Hello Elisabeth, please may I see the General?"

She put a finger to her lips for shhhh,

"He is in his bed, follow me."

Hareclough Heights

Chapter 7

FAILING HEALTH

I went back to the stable to brush Caper, but one of the lads had done it for me.

Elsie will be back any time, so I collected Peggy, and we walked up the lane to meet her.

The doctor's limousine passed us going down the track, and he waved.

"Hello, you two kept people as I work, how has your day been?"

I wept as I told her, and it made Elsie weep too.

"I told dad straight away, and he has gone to see him, and as Peggy and I were walking up to meet you, the doctor's car went down. The General`s car arrived this morning. What a beauty, just like the ones I drove in the war, when needed. I offered him the car or the trap, and he chose the trap; we then went to our piece of land. He said he loved it too."

This is going to be a sad time for us all, Elsie, and we have to be the strong ones for mum and dad and Elisabeth. Let's get all our crying done on the way home."

"You are such an emotional darling, just like me, and I love you so much, it hurts."

We did as we said; we cried and sobbed, then we were alright, and then we sobbed and cried again.

Peggy was looking at us with his head tilting from side to side, unable to understand. I am not sure we do.

Dad was coming out of the House as we got home.

"Thank you for telling me, son, as we have thought for a while, the General has pneumonia and is heading away from us."

"Was it the trenches?"

"He could never know for certain but thinks almost certainly."

We could see my dad was upset, so we let him go and see mum and share their upcoming grief like we did.

A room had been made in the old wood store to garage the car, so I went to put it away.

"Edward?"

"Yes, Elisabeth, how may I help you?"

"First of all, I want to thank you so much for the time you afforded Edward these past few months."

"No problem at all, I assure you, I love him as my second dad."

"He talks of the time of his time with you and your father and how close he became to you over the 6 years you all spent together. Did he tell you I was not able to have a child?"

"No, never, he just said you were never blessed with children."

"He was never a man to cosset anything apart from you, Edward, and when your dad asked if he and your mum could call you Edward, he was overjoyed and felt you loved him as he loved you."

"That is very true, Elisabeth. I would have given my life for him."

She began to sob, and I pulled her towards me.

"He is worth your tears, no disgrace in crying, he is a great man with a fantastic legacy to leave on the world."

"Thank you, Edward. I can see why you so took him."

"You are very kind."

"Were you about to garage his motor car?"

"Yes, I was."

"Maybe leave it out so he can see it if we ever get it out again."

"Absolutely. May I call in to see him on Thursday? He may feel like a ride in his car, or in the trap, I know he may not, but it's worth asking?"

"Anytime you wish, open house to your family."

Martin told me about the decline in the General's health. We owe that family so much for all they have done for us, Martin and me, and for Martin before me.

We were rushing toward Christmas and the New Year; well, it sure felt that way. It did not get proper light in the morning till after 8.00, and was now dark by 4.00

The mums or dads or someone took the children up for the bus around 8.20 and then went to meet them about 3.30

"Elisabeth said she was glad she got electricity all over the buildings while you were all away."

"Me too, of course, we had candlelight most of the time away in the war."

"She said it was their bit towards keeping people in work, and most of the wiring was done by young ladies, some of whom offered more than just lighting us up, or so she believed."

"Did Elisabeth ever say how they got this place?"

"Of course, she and the General came from almost the Aristocracy."

"Almost, how can you be almost an Aristocrat?"

"Let me finish, Martin."

"Yes, of course, dear, another glass of port, to help you think?"

"Are you trying to get me tipsy? I have already had one glass?"

"Just one for me then."

"Don't put words into my mouth, or anything else, perhaps a small one."

"As if I would try that old trick,"

"Anyway, her true Uncle was the Earl of Baldersly, and the General's true uncle was Lord Alberson.

They are the fourth generation of Cartwrights to own Hareclough Hall. As far as she knows, they have no close family to inherit."

"That is very interesting, hope whoever inherits has a liking for game."

"Do not worry, love, you will always work. You look tired."

"Not really, I am alright."

"Perhaps you did not hear me right, YOU LOOK TIRED."

"Yawns, you know what?"

This Saturday was November 5th, and in the UK, we call it Bonfire Night.

History tells us that on this day in 1605, a group of men tried to blow up the House of Lords during the state opening of Parliament, which was called The Gunpowder Treason Plot.

Guy Fawkes headed the crew, and his team were fellow Catholic dissidents from the Midlands of England.

The plot was thwarted, and after weeks of torturous questioning, only two of the group confessed. Guy Fawkes, the so-called leader, was tried for treason, for which there was only one sentence: hanged, drawn and quartered.

He was executed on January 31st, 1606, in the Tower of London.

To celebrate his demise, we have big bonfires and special treats every November 5th, including toffee, ginger biscuits, dark golden parkin, and other sweet treats.

Parkin was regionalized in Yorkshire; here is Granny D's recipe.

225g/8oz Butter

225g/8oz Soft brown sugar

2 beaten eggs

350g/12oz Plain flour

225g/8oz Black treacle

2tbsp Ground ginger

2tbsp Ground cinnamon

Pinch of salt

1tsp Bicarbonate of soda

250ml/1/2 Pint warm milk

Line 10" square tin with greaseproof paper

Melt together slowly the treacle, sugar, and butter, and keep stirring constantly.

Remove from the heat and add the beaten eggs.

Stir in salt, cinnamon and ginger into the melted mixture.

In a new bowl, add the bicarbonate of soda and mix in the milk.

Add the treacle mixture and mix well

Add to the square tin.

Warm the oven to the temperature.

Bake in a Fan Oven @ 128* for 1 to 1 ¼ hours.

Bake in a gas oven at 350°F for 1 to 1 ¼ hours.

Allow it to coon, then remove from the tin and cut into thick slices.

Spread with good butter and eat,

Store in an airtight tin.

"I could just eat some Parkin now."

We built a bonfire in the middle of the field next to the House.

Every single bit of wood, paper, and rubbish was burnt.

We usually have fireworks, but decided against it this year; however, the House provided lots of sparklers.

Everyone was there, I even wheeled out the General onto his raised patio to watch and saved him some of the parkin mum had made.

"Wednesday is a School day and one I was looking forward to.

Great students, yes, but not that, you would never guess why it was Elsie."

"Is this one of your riddles, Edward?"

"Afraid so, love."

"Let me guess, beef stew for lunch."

"So very close."

"I give in."

"Jam Roly Poly and custard for pudding."

"I do love you, Edward Daniels."

"Enough to give me your Roly Poly Pudding at lunch time?"

"No."

Hahahahaha

We got on the bus with the children from the House Estate who quickly mingled with the rest of the children going to school. Their chatter was so funny sometimes.

"I swallowed mum's sixpence by accident."

"Did you get clattered?"

"Not straight away, no."

"Why, what did she do?"

"Gave me a spoonful of Castra Oil"

"Oh yuck, were you sick?"

"No, she sat me on Katy`s potty till I did my business."

"And, did you?"

"Oh yes, I did alright."

"Were you allowed to keep the sixpence as a memento?"

"No, it is buying tonight`s tea."

"Then what?"

"The I got battered."

He laughed, they laughed, and Elsie and I laughed.

A nightmare at lunchtime, I read the menus wrong. Jam Roly Poly was yesterday's pudding. The consolation was that it was Spotted Dick and custard, my second favourite.

"What did you have for pudding yesterday, Elsie?"

"You know, I really don`t remember Roly, I mean Edward."

It was pouring with rain when we got off the bus, and we were all soaked through to our skins.

Not sure how the worker's family managed, but undressing naked on our doorstep certainly had its ups. As we progressed to the kitchen and.........

After our joint bath, we dried each other in a deathly silence, just looking at each other, and enjoying what we saw.

"I do love you, Edward Daniels."

"Yes, I can see why!"

"Will you still love me when I am fat, Edward?"

"You are as skinny as a stick, love."

"But will you still love me when I am fat?"

"I think you are trying to tell me something, darling?"

"I may be."

"Can I have another clue, please?"

"My knee touched his thingy."

"Where does that go?"

"I knew you would do something like that. Sorry, I love you so much, Elsie Daniels, and am I right?"

"Absolutely."

We cuddled, stood on our towels, naked in the bathroom.

"It obviously excited you, Edward."

"I am a bloke; It takes very little to excite me, my darling. Could I possibly invite you to join me in bed and be loved as you deserve?"

"I am a girl; it takes very little to persuade me, my darling."

Teatime, and we were going to my mum and dad`s.

"Did you enjoy your Jam Roly Poly, Edward?"

"It was on the menu yesterday, mum, someone at this table had it and never told me."

"How could you keep a secret like that from him, Elsie?"

"Pretty easy, I am really good with secrets, Granny."

The table erupted, and tears of joy flowed.

Dad and Paul kissed us and shook our hands.

"Have you a date yet, Elsie?"

"No mum, but I reckon I am about 14 weeks."

Mum took the calendar off the wall.

"What is today`s date?"

"December 2nd, Mum."

"That would make it about the end of August and the beginning of September."

After tea, we went to the big house to share our news with them.

"Hello, you two, quick, come in out of the cold."

"Thank you, Elisabeth, is it me or the General or even both of us you want?"

"Both please, is the General up for visitors?"

"Yes, I am sure he is. Come through. Darling, Edward and Elsie are visiting."

"How wonderful, thank, cough, cough, you for thinking to call."

"We have some news we wish to share with you, being our adopted family."

"We love news, don`t we, dear, excellent news."

The General nodded and smiled.

"We wish to announce we are having a baby."

"Wonderful news, Edward, any dates, Elsie?"

"Yes, next August/September time."

"We are so happy, cough, cough, for you both, the best news I have heard, cough, cough, for ages, thank you for telling us."

"I agree, Edward, we feel blessed to be told, and your feelings for us as family, thank you."

We sat with them for an hour and saw that the General was tiring.

"I will see you tomorrow, good night to you both."

"The same to you two, thank you so much for calling with your fabulous news, we both love you so much."

We kissed cheeks and went home to share our news with Peggy.

"We have some news for you, Peggy, mummy is going to give you a brother or sister next year, isn`t that just wonderful news?"

She licked Elsie's face.

"Do you really think she knows what we say, Elsie?"

"I am positive she does, don`t you?"

"Not sure."

Peggy came back in. She had been upstairs, and she brought in Froggy. She placed it on my knee and rested her head there, too.

"Yes, I do now, Elsie, cup of tea?"

"Please."

The weather was decidedly chilly outside now, but I had said I would see if the General wanted to go out.

"Good morning Elisabeth, is the General taking visitors today?"

"Only you, your dad and the doctor."

"Good morning, Sir, would you fancy a jaunt out in your car? It is far too cold for the trap."

"Do you know, son, I do believe I do."

"Excellent, give me 10 minutes to warm her up, Sir."

"What did he say?"

"Yes, so I am just going to warm him up and make a flask of tea."

"Leave the tea to me."

I was soon back, and he had his oversized coat on and a woolly deerstalker.

"Darling?"

"Yes, my love."

"May I come with you?"

"Yes, of course, nothing, cough, cough, cough, would give me greater pleasure, my dear."

We all got in the car and off we went up the lane.

"Shall we go to Blackpool or Scarborough, Edward?"

"Perhaps a compromise, Sir, how does Hareclough Heights sound?"

"Perfect, dear boy, cough, cough, cough, just perfect."

We were overlooking the valley on Hareclough Heights in 10 minutes.

"How lucky are we, Elsabeth, to be able to live here?"

"We certainly are, darling, a cup of tea?"

"That, cough, cough, would be delightful, thank you."

"And perhaps a slice of the cook's own recipe fruit cake and cheese?"

"Once again, you spoil me, cough, cough, my dear."

Elisabeth had packed up her picnic hamper. How lovely.

"See the big house over there, Edward, cough, cough?"

"Yes, I do, Sir."

"Hareclough House, it is where, cough, cough, I live now."

"Do you see the big, cough, cough, spire, Edward?"

"Yes, I do, Sir."

"Well, boy, that is where I am heading, and, cough, cough, pretty soon too, I would say."

"Please do not talk like that, dear, you have lots of time yet."

"Elisabeth, it would be nice when I am gone, cough, cough, to have a seat placed on this very spot we are in now."

"Of course, my darling, and perhaps Edward could keep running me up to sit and talk to you."

The general never answered; he just nodded, and we all had tears running down our faces.

"Home, I think Edward, I am, cough, cough, feeling tired."

"Yes, of course, Sir."

"Another slice of cake, Edward?"

We both answered yes.

I helped him out of the car and back into his chair.

"Edward?"

"Yes, Sir?"

"Unless Elizabeth needs to use the car, I want you to drive it; they need running daily, cough, cough, not stuck in a garage all week, so please treat her as your own."

"I do not know what to say, Sir. Are you sure?"

"I owe you and your dad, cough, a lot more than a car, Cough, cough."

"Thank you, Sir, may I pick Elsie and the children up from the bus stop tonight?"

He was exhausted and just nodded.

"Thank you for the sightseeing journey, Edward, you are very kind."

"You two are also my family, Elsabeth."

We kissed each other's cheeks, and I left her in tears.

Mum was just on her way home from her needlework.

"Mum?"

She looked around.

"Hello, darling."

"If you have a few minutes, could you pop in and see Elisabeth? I left her quite tearful."

I explained what had happened over the past few hours, and Mum went to the House.

Mum said Elisabeth had mixed emotions, sad at the Generals' fast decline and over the moon with our news.

When she left, around 8.00, they were both going to bed.

They did not have far to travel; they had converted the second drawing room into their bedroom, so they never had to go up and down the stairs.

The doctor had prescribed a powder to mix with water to help the General sleep, and it worked perfectly.

December was a magical month for all, as the workers in the fields had it much earlier and took on odd jobs around the house, since all the farm work was done by spring.

Roofs were repaired, door hinges were reset, and painting was done in the big house. They also created decorations for the Christmas tree in the yard and candle holders to adorn the tree.

For the wives, they had their men close by and had time for themselves when the children went to school.

It was no coincidence that many of the children had birthdays in September.

Not forgetting the children who had lots of Christmas wishes and lovely chores.

They created a Christmas card for their mothers, fathers, and loved ones. Christmas decorations were to be cut out and stuck together, and letters were to be written to Santa Claus.

The General and Elisabeth always gave the workers a cash Christmas bonus of some size three weeks before Christmas, enabling them to buy presents. All the presents could be stored in the dining room, and the table could be used for wrapping the presents. It was such a happy time.

"Edward?"

"Yes, Dad?"

"Have you chosen the Christmas tree for the yard and House, and one each for us two?"

"Yes, Sir, and they are coming down in the morning."

"Good, I want the yard one decorated to suit a King."

"I understand, Sir, we won't let you down."

Chapter 8

SAD TIMES

"Quick, Edward, look outside, 3 days to Christmas, and it`s beginning to snow."

"Perfect timing, you, me, and the children all finished school, I may play out with the kids later if it gets deeper."

"Play out!"

"I meant to show how to build a snowman and make snowballs."

"Snowballs, you said, let me look upstairs and see if I can warm any up."

"I may have to come and help."

"Perfect, you stop down here, Peggy and guard."

She opened one eye and went back to sleep,

"It has got deeper, and such a blizzard you can not see a thing outside."

I opened the door for Peggy to go out. She sniffed a little, rushed out, had a pee, and rushed back into her basket.

"Would you like a cuddle and your belly rubbed?"

"Not you, Elsie, then again."

Too late, Peggy Woo was on the settee and rolled onto her back.

"You can be next, Elsie."

"I do not mind being second to a dumb animal."

"Shh, she will hear you."

"I wasn`t talking to Peggy!"

"I will go get some logs from the barn to keep us warm."

"You are desperate to play out, aren't you, Edward?"

"Maybe, desperate is a strong word, then again, yes."

We had a handcrafted, beautiful wood store for logs and kindling, which was connected to a gorgeous day kennel and run. However, there was also Peggy.

I am not saying she ate it, but she certainly chewed it. Not to escape, she slept on the concrete area it was built on. Three times, she demolished it. I wonder why Labradors love chewing.

Edward brought in a basketful of logs, so we should be fine for a bit.

"Just going back out for a while, love, the children asked if I wanted to play out, I could not say no, well, could I?"

"No love, let me do your jacket up, there, have you got a clean hankie?"

"Yes, thank you, I will be back before the streetlights come on."

Hahahahaha.

I put on my oversized coat and went to work, only across the yard, but being pregnant, Edward came along with me.

I was helping cook this morning, basting the Christmas cakes we made last month with Brandy, making some mince pies and a few jam tarts.

No real house gossip, but we took 2 hours talking about it anyway!

In the few hours I spent with the cook, Edward, and his playmates, they had built a family of snowmen.

"Are you going home, love?"

"Not quite yet, just popping in to see Elisabeth and maybe Edward."

"Come in, Elsie, how are you doing in the snow with such a precious cargo on board?"

"Hello Elisabeth, Edward is my chaperone in the snow, he is playing out with the kids at present, building snowmen."

"Bless him, cup of tea?"

"No, I am ok, thank you, I need the toilet enough at the moment, just checking on how you are both doing."

"Oh, I am doing fine, thank you. Edward is not so good today; he sleeps more and more."

"And that bothers you, not at all?"

"I would not say that, no."

"So how are you at the moment, Elisabeth?"

"Absolutely awful love."

"As I thought. I cannot imagine your mind."

"I am so deeply sad, inside Elsie and do not know what to do."

"Maybe walk around the House a little, see what people are doing, maybe help them."

"Yes, I probably could, thank you."

"Also, and very importantly, start making plans. Sounds harsh, but you will have enough on your mind soon enough."

"Very true, and I will."

We cuddled and both cried,

"I will call my chaperone now, Elisabeth, bless him. Look at him, he is in a snowball fight, sighs. Call in anytime with me or mum for a tea and a chat."

"I will, my love, I promise."

"Edward?"

"Just coming, please wait there."

"Thank you, darling."

"How is the General?"

"Elisabeth said he is fading by the day."

"That is so sad, so sad for a lot of people."

"I know love, back safe from the greatest war ever, but taken down by those dank trenches."

"I will call in and see him soon."

"Is it in time now, Edward? Can I run you a nice hot and bubbly bath with a fat wench washing you down?"

"No, thank you."

"Oh."

"Only joking, of course you may, it is what wenches are all about."

"I do hope you will not take advantage of me, Sir."

"I may, I may not, it just depends."

"On what, Sir?"

"If there was enough room for a Sir and a fat wench."

"I could always sit on your knee, Sir."

"Elsie Daniels!"

"Christmas Eve 1947, and at home with my dear wife and family, how marvellous is that Dora?"

"Almost a miracle, Martin."

"Who had the right to split families up from their husbands and fathers?"

"A mad man, Dora, a mad man."

The week before Christmas, all the tenant farmers and workforce gather in the stock barn for a Christmas drink or two. Martin said all appeared to be upset at the news of the General, and some tears were shed.

Cook had provided seasonal treats, such as Christmas and mince pies.

On Christmas day, as always, it was a pleasure looking out over the yard at the children, in their best clothes, playing out with the simplest of toys and having fun.

The snow had almost gone now, just small piles of white snow with the odd carrot nose on the floor.

I had asked Elisabeth if she and the General would like to join us for Christmas Day Dinner, but she declined only because she knew he was now on borrowed time.

Martin was exhausted with his workload, as he and Paul had been with puppies being picked up for the past two weeks before Christmas, which were being given as presents to loved ones. Plus, all the figures needed for the year-end stocktake.

"What can I do to help mum? I have prepared all the vegetables last night?"

"Not much to do really, the turkey has been on a low light all night, when that comes out, the pork goes in. I will put the Christmas pudding into the steamer 3 hours before we want it, so all is currently in hand."

"It was kind of you to invite my mum and dad down for Christmas dinner."

"Never a problem, Elsie, they, like you, are lovely people."

Different households have different ways they use presents. When we had children, it was always a stocking at the end of their bed, which, when thinking about it, will start again next Christmas when we have Junior Davies with us.

Now we exchange gifts after we have had our Christmas dinner.

With my needlework skills, I bought white hankies for each one, and embroidered them with their initial on one corner and a flower or animal on the other. I loved them so much that I made three hankies for myself as well.

Edward, Elsie, and Peggy came through at mid-morning, and Elsie's parents, Brian and Claire, arrived around 12, just after Paul and

Martin returned from the kennels and washed up presentable.

Peggy is now looking her age, at nearly 10 years old. Martin says she has lived an extraordinary life here with us all, but Labs don't have a long lifespan; working labs typically don't live much past 8.

"Thank you for the invitation, Dora; it was very kind of you."

"You are both more than welcome, Claire. We do not socialize enough, and Christmas on your own must be like any other day."

"Very true, sometimes we just do not bother."

"All still doing well on the farm, Brian?"

"Yes, Martin, it has been an excellent year, both crops and animals."

"The hogg and lamb you sent down were delicious."

"Thank you, can you believe the first was over 2 years ago?"

"Incredible how time flies when you are in a normal living life, when we were away, a day felt like a week."

"How is the General, Martin? The reports I had were very gloomy."

"He is not good, Brian, not good at all. We all fear the worst at any time. He had ended up with nasty pneumonia, and his lungs were so bad that he had no way of fighting it."

"I agree, unfortunate news indeed."

"Dora asked them here too for Christmas dinner, but Elisabeth said, as this was probably the last one they would have together, she wanted it at home."

"Yes, I can see that, we will pray for them both come Sunday."

"Can everyone sit down, please, just this chair for Martin so he has elbow room to carve.

We should just about finish for the King's Christmas speech."

Martin carved the turkey; it was from a neighbouring farm on the estate and given to us as a present for all Paul and Martin do for them.

It must have been a 14-pounder; it had to be almost forced into the oven.

When we're done, I will pack Brian and Claire a good wedge of it to take home, plus bits of all sorts to make a dinner for tomorrow for them, or, since it's Boxing Day, invite them down again. I love a house full.

In 1947, we had ration books to buy food. We were lucky as the farmers on the estate gave us plenty, and the cook just happened to have some spare Christmas pudding mix.

3.00 And we listened to our King. The men all stood to listen. He spoke sincerely, as if addressing each of us individually.

I poured us all a Port, and we drank his health, Elsie pretended to, and Martin drank hers.

We played what we called parlour games, such as Charades, I Spy, Hunt the Thimble, and 20 Questions, that sort of thing. It gave us lots of fun and laughs.

Brian and Dora began to get ready to go home at around 5.00.

"Please stay for tea, you two, we have lots of leftovers and a few new additions."

"We feel as we have presumed on you all too long.

"Please stay a little longer, mummy and me and Edward will take you home in the Humber."

"Only if you are really sure, is that ok with you, Brian?"

"Yes, for sure it is good to be in such a loving family, thank you."

So we all carried on playing until I slipped away and got out the extras, such as boiled eggs, cheese, buns, mince pies, and Christmas cake.

I loved a family get-together, but we didn't have enough; however, we will from now on.

We continued to eat leftovers for the next two days. Then I boiled the turkey bones with the neck and liver, mixed with carrots, onions, and potatoes, and that, along with bread, fed us for the next two days.

As I was leaving the house a few days later, I was asked to deliver a message to Martin.

He was wanted at the House, not urgent, but when he had time, if he was wanted, it was always urgent to him under the present circumstances."

"Hello Elisabeth, Dora said when I get a moment, I am wanted."

"Yes, Martin, Edward said he wanted a chat."

"How is he, Elisabeth?"

"Nearing the end, I fear Martin."

She began to cry, and I pulled her onto my shoulder.

"Thank you, Martin, you are very kind."

"Good afternoon, General, good to see you keeping warm, Sir."

"Yes, I am Martin, cough, she spoils me."

"And rightly so, Sir, if you are not worth it, no one else is."

"Could you or Edward take me on a little ride tomorrow, now that the snow is clearing?"

"Of course, Sir, would you prefer morning or the afternoon?"

"cough, if it is dry and clear in the morning and you do not have a lot to drink, cough, cough, it being New Year's Eve, then, or in the afternoon if it is, cough, not clear.

"My late night on New Year's Eve is a thing of the past, Sir."

"Elisabeth, cough, cough, will pack a snack up and tea, cough, and will be coming with us."

"No problem at all, Sir, it will be like old times, as unhappy as they are to remember.

Everything on the estate is running as it should. All seven farms are producing as they should, with yields higher than last year and all rent up to date."

Elisabeth showed me out and we hugged.

At teatime, I told Dora, Edward and Elsie exactly what was said.

"Where did you take the General, Edward?"

"In good weather, in the trap to where we hope to build one day overlooking the River Tauper. In good weather, up to Hareclough Heights overlooking the town."

"Do you want to come, Edward?"

"Yes, please, something is telling me I need to."

"Let us all celebrate New Year's Eve this evening. Are you playing with the rest of our fellow workers, musicians Edward?"

"Yes, mum, guitar, we won't take the piano out, too heavy, and it loses its tune."

"How so, Edward?"

"The different climate, warm in here and cold outside, contracts the strings inside."

"Well, you learn something new every day."

"Will you and your bump be singing Elsie?"

"Probably a few like, Let it snow, Chestnut's roasting on an open fire, and We`ll meet again, don`t know where, don`t know when. Depends on the wind."

"What wind?"

"My wind from our bump."

We all worked on the trap and carriage barn, most of the bunting from the store barn, and removed some of the tree decorations. We did not use open flames, as it was a bit dangerous in such a small area, but we did light four braziers to keep warm and roast chestnuts, as well as bake some potatoes.

We invited Brian and Claire down again. Paul said he would sleep in the lounge so they could have his bed. He is such a thoughtful and kind young man. I wish he would meet his one somewhere, but I have no idea where, as he never goes out.

It was a lovely night; Elsie's bump was good, and she sang during the night, then led us all in 'Auld Lang Syne'.

On the stroke of midnight, a couple of the farm boys set off 10 rockets that the House had donated for our night.

As we were all looking up, a young servant tripped in front of Paul, and he caught her in a rather unfortunate area.

"Sorry, Sir, for being so careless. I was looking up instead of where I was going."

"And I am sorry for manhandling you where I did; I usually leave that area for the third or fourth date."

She giggled.

"Sir, I am Lorna. Will we have another date, just asking?"

"Yes, I do think we may. I am Paul. Would you like to stand with me?"

"If I may, Sir, I hardly know anyone here, Brrrrr."

"You are cold, take my coat."

"Oh, I couldn`t, Sir, Brrrrr, I will go in if I may, Sir."

"Please call me Paul, and let`s put my coat over us both and cuddle."

She giggled again, and they cuddled.

I was so happy to see Paul happy, and she's just a slip of a girl. I will ask the cook about her tomorrow.

And tomorrow it was already, January 1st, 1948

By 8 am, the sun was beginning to come over Hareclough Heights, so it looked as though Martin would be taking the General for his New Year's ride.

"Happy New Year, Elisabeth. How are you both this morning?"

"Much the same, thank you for asking, Martin."

"We have all day if he feels like his ride."

"Let us say 10.00, Martin, any different and I will let you know."

"Perfect, is it ok if Edward comes along?"

"Yes, of course, he is very welcome."

I kissed her cheek and cuddled her.

I went down to our New Year's Eve store to help tidy up and get the trap and carriage back in.

Paul was there with Laura; she had been given time off to help.

"This is my brother Edward, Laura."

"Very pleased to meet you, Sir."

"And I, you, Laura."

Mum had found out from the cook that Laura was 20+ years old and had lived with her grandmother, who thought it was time she was in service and learned some discipline, as in routine.

My brother was indeed smitten, and about time too. Paul is an absolute gentleman in every way and a lovely man, to boot.

I brought the car around and right in front of the House.

"Would you care to travel in the back or front, General?"

"Back with, cough cough, Elisabeth, please.

"Yes, Sir, our pleasure."

I opened the back door and helped the General into the back of the car.

Elisabeth got into the car through the other door, and they linked up.

Edward and I jumped in, and off we went. We followed the farm track towards the river.

"Cough, cough, cough."

We sat a while and waited for instructions.

"Why here, Martin?"

"Cough, cough, cough."

"Edward showed the General where we would love to live, overlooking the river Tauper and the sandy bank we enjoyed growing up."

"Us too, Martin, unless that is too hard to believe?"

"Cough, cough, cough."

"Not at all, Elisabeth."

The general tapped the back of my seat, and I turned round and back up the track we drove.

"Cough, cough, cough."

Through the town, passed the school and church and climbed the hill up to Hareclough Heights.

We took a right along the moor top road.

"Next left, Dad, to the end of the road."

"Cough, cough, cough."

"Just here."

"If you look down here, Ma'am, you can just make out the beach and the track to Hareclough House, the church, school and sports field."

Dad tapped my leg and put a finger to his lips.

We heard sniffling in the back, so I slowly turned around and made my way back into town.

Elisabeth tapped me on my shoulder.

"Hospital, please, Martin."

"On my way."

I went into the casualty and explained the situation, and they came out with a trolley and took the General inside with Elisabeth holding the trolley.

"Please go back, Martin. I will sort out transport."

"I will take Edward back and come back and wait for you."

"I will stay with you, Dad, if I may."

"Elisabeth nodded and went into the hospital."

"I will just go ring mum, won`t be long.!

"Please ask her to let Elsie know."

We both needed a little time to ourselves. The General was a very special person in both our lives.

Hareclough Heights

Chapter 9

NEW ARRIVAL

Unfortunate times at Hareclough House, although expected to be heartbreaking all the same.

Edward and I drove home, each with our own thoughts of the war years—the absolute heartbreak of losing members of our force to the rival enemy force. The cold and hunger we all suffered, as officers, we took no extra rations.

The laughs we shared in the good times, and yes, we had good times, maybe not as bad as others.

Under General Edward Cartwright, we were all as safe as we could be, taking into account we were in World War 11 and were being bombarded with bullets and bombs, and were returning bullets and bombs.

After we helped win the war, our General retired from the services and took on the honourable title of Field Marshal, but was always addressed as General to the rank and file of his loyal men.

"I see you two are alone, Martin."

"Yes, as the coughing in the back seat stopped, I realized we had lost him, Dora."

"Where is Elisabeth?"

"Still at the hospital with the General."

"Would you take me to her, please?"

"Yes, of course, you get out now, Edward and tell Elsie."

"Ok, Dad, will you 2 be alright? I do not mind coming with you."

"We will be fine, thank you, son."

I felt I needed to be with Elisabeth; we were the nearest to family they ever had. As compassionate as men can be, she needs another woman to cry with.

"Thank you, Martin, I can manage now."

"Ring me to pick you up."

"Yes, of course, thank you."

The hospital was very quiet, as if in the memory of a brave man.

"Excuse me, I am looking for Mrs. Cartwright; her deceased husband came in earlier."

"Let me take you to her love. I am glad she now has company."

I followed the Sister to a side room, she knocked, and I went in.

I held out my arms, and Elisabeth accepted my invitation. Sister closed the door, and we cried as one, and we stayed in the embrace.

Sister brought us cups of tea, and we sat down, just holding hands.

"Martin will come for us when you are ready, Elisabeth."

"Maybe now, Dora, please, I am done here."

Sister let me use her phone, and Martin was with us within 15 minutes. We had walked to the reception to wait for him. He parked right outside, and we went out to meet him..

I sat in the back with Elisabeth.

"Would you like to stay with us tonight, Elisabeth?"

"Thank you, Dora. I will be fine, thank you, but if anything changes, may I call you?"

"Of course, at any time."

I accompanied her into the House, and a couple of the house staff took over from me.

Martin put the car away, and we walked the short distance home, arm in arm.

We both had a restless night, tossing and turning; we were glad of a bit of daylight so we could get up.

Martin took on the household duties and rang his old army camp, and they made all the necessary arrangements, liaising, of course, with Elisabeth.

At teatime, Martin had been contacted.

"Yes, Dora, the army camp contacted me and said he would be buried with full military honours on the 12th of January 1948.

They asked if you and I would be Pole Bearers, Edward. I said I would ask you."

"Yes, of course, Sir."

"They would supply four more. They wanted me to speak to Elisabeth for her agreement."

"Would you like me to do that, Martin?"

" Yes, please, Dora, thank you."

"I thought it was quiet. Where is Peggy?"

"Well, mum told her what we were doing and ignored us. I left the door open in case she changed her mind."

"How is your friend doing, Paul?"

"She is doing extremely wonderfully, thank you, Edward."

"I was not prying, Paul, but my how you have changed these last few days."

"That is good, Edward, I have to say, I am deeply in love with the little servant girl.

Would you say, and be honest, that with me being five or six years older, it is too much?"

"No, not at all, dear Paul, that's from a girl's point of view."

"Thank you, Elsie."

"I will pop down and see she is ok, Elsie."

"Thank you, Edward, you are such a love."

It was strange, I couldn`t hear anything.

Oh, poor darling Peggy was still in her basket, motionless; we had lost her. I could not hold back my tears.

"Are you ok, Edward?"

I could not answer. I heard footsteps, and Elsie was at my side. She joined in my tears.

She knelt beside Peggy.

"Look, Edward, she went up for Froggy."

Edward came back up to tell us all about Peggy, our second death in two days. Again, we were all heartbroken.

The day after Edward dug a grave in the doggy graveyard, which was set up especially for the dogs.

Sweet Peggy was laid to rest with Froggy, and she was buried with few words but lots of heavy hearts.

It was not long before the newspapers wanted to interview Elisabeth, Martin and Edward.

The army set up a time for the day after for any journalists and the three interviewees.

They spoke to Elisabeth about her and the General; she was very assured and well spoken.

"Now, Martin, what can you tell us from WW1 about you being given the Victoria Cross for bravery?"

The family and Elisabeth sat with open mouths; they had no idea what was going on.

"I was just doing my duty, we were under heavy fire and when we got back into the trenches, no General.

I looked out and saw him on the floor. I watched for a while and saw him move. I stripped to my vest and ran back towards the enemy. I put him over my shoulders and brought him home. He has sprained his knee and ankle and cannot stand."

We were all dumbfounded that one of our family members had received the Victoria Cross, the highest award in the world for valour.

"Moving on, if we may, Edward, what can you tell us about being your Victoria Cross?"

This must be a dream, a lovely dream at that.

"Martin, I whispered, is this true?"

"Yes, love, shhh."

"Like my father, we were under intense fire, and we moved forward to take out a sniper point, but it was a trap, and a whole bunch of them opened fire on us.

I saw many a good soldier killed outright, and a private was shot but was still alive. I put him over my shoulder and carried him back to our trenches, and looked back at the carnage unfolding.

I saw another young private hit and moving, so I ran back, put him over my shoulder and got back into he trenches. Both lads were wounded in several places but pulled through; for them, their war was over.

Again, the family and Elisabeth are full of open mouths.

"Last question from us, if we can, why did you never go to Buckingham Palace and have them presented?"

"We reckoned they had enough medals to hand out, and one day we would be called."

The day after, the newspapers were full of the news that a father and son in different wars had won a Victorious Cross.

All enquiries had to go through the Ministry of Defence, so we could be left alone to bury our dead.

On the morning of the General's funeral, we had several army visitors, including one who told us all, including Elisabeth, who was at our house.

"The Field Marshal shall be brought home.

The Field Marshal will leave his home in an Army Hearse, which will take him as far as the outskirts of town.

The Field Marshal will then be transferred to a horse-drawn gun Carriage and will lead a Battalion of soldiers and the family mourners, the half mile to the church.

Family mourners can ride or walk.

The Field Marshal will be carried into the church by six pallbearers in full military uniform, as previously warned, into the church.

After the Service, His Royal Highness the King will say a few words before joining the Funeral Cortège to the graveside.

The Union Jack covering the casket will be presented to you, Ma'am, as next of kin.

The Field Marshal will be lowered into his grave, and a firing party will perform a 3-volley salute.

A bugler will play "Taps" in military Style.

We will then all go into the church hall for a small wake, where His Royal Highness the

King will present the two Victoria Crosses simultaneously to the Father and Son who bravely put their own lives at risk to save others.

The Battalion will then be stood down, and His Highness will depart for the sports club to retrieve his helicopter and return to London.

Any questions?"

There was not one; we were all still in shock for all the reasons listed above.

"I will see you all just before 11.00, not sure if the King will be here or joining us en route. See you all soon, and please relax as we say goodbye to one of us."

He saluted and left us.

"Martin Davies, in here, a word."

"Edward Davies, in here, a word."

I think Elsie and I asked the same questions.

"Darling, why would you not tell your family of your great honour?"

"A simple answer, my darling, the great wars were not about us at all. We were the lucky ones; it was the ones who died who were the heroes. They gave their lives for King and country."

I just cuddled him; I was so proud of all my family.

The army arrived just after 10.30 with the General`s casket draped in the Union Jack, in the back of the military Hearst.

Transport for the Family and Senior House, as well as farmhands, was provided by the army; all we had to do was get in.

"Will you share this one with Martin and me, Elisabeth?"

"Thank you, Dora. I was worried I would be alone."

"You will never be alone as long as we are here, love, please bear that in mind."

"Was I imagining it, or did he really say the King would be present?"

"Yes, he did, what an honour for you, Elisabeth."

"Well, yes, and Martin?"

"Yes, Elisabeth."

"Thank you for saving my Edwards' life."

"Thank you, Elisabeth and you are so very welcome. He was the best leader in the Army."

And off we went, probably the worst few hours in Elisabeth`s life, but we are all here for her.

"Captain Martin Davies was awarded the Victoria Cross for saving the life of his commanding officer. Please walk towards His Majesty.

Lieutenant Edward Davies was awarded the Victoria Cross for saving two lives of his company under enemy fire. Please walk towards His Majesty.

I noticed Paul was crying through both ceremonies. I am so glad he never went to war.

Looking back over the first three quarters or so of 1948, I have mixed emotions.

Elisabeth and I have become closer and closer, and I give her the support and love I would give a sister.

We now have happier times to look forward to. Paul and Laura are an item, and she is lovely, just right for our Paul.

In the next month or so, we are expecting our first grandchild, Martin, and I cannot wait.

I know we lost our darling Peggy, and poor Elsie was heartbroken over her loss.

Paul says he will give them a new puppy when she has her baby, so that they can grow up together, which is a good idea. He said he has a direct relation with her old Peggy, due in November.

"How does it feel, Mrs Davies, to be finishing work for 3 months or so to have our baby?"

"Had it not been for the war, this may have been our second or third child, Edward."

"Very true love, are you worried about it?"

"No, not at all after what you have been through, my darling, I feel it's my duty to us."

"Good, brave, girl, I do love you so."

"Mum?"

"Yes Elsie?"

"Whatever do you find yourself doing all day at home?

"You will soon find out when our little one arrives, love."

"I was not being silly inquisitive, it`s just I do not feel like doing anything."

Hahahahaha

The workers were home for tea; it was all ready to serve.

"Owwwwwww."

"You ok, Elsie?"

"I have this pain in my tummy, do you think our baby could be coming early?"

"Oh, I do hope so, love, we so need something new in all our lives."

"Just you sit quietly and see if you can eat some tea, Elsie."

"Ok, mum."

I served up, and I could tell by Elsie's face that her labour had begun.

We all ate up, and Elsie, as always, washed and dried the dishes.

"You ok, Elsie?"

"Yes, OWWWWW."

"It`s ok, love, Edward will take you to the hospital now you have had your tea."

"Yes, I will go get the car."

I helped her outside. She did not need help, but it was all new to her, and as I expected, her waters broke as we waited for Edward.

"Oh no."

"It's ok, love, only your waters broken, you will still be hours before junior arrives."

"Thank you, mum."

"Would you like me to ring your mum to come to the hospital?"

"Yes, please."

I could see her eyes filling up.

"You will be brilliant, love, don`t worry."

"No rush, Edward, no need to speed."

"Thank you, mum."

"Hello Claire, Edward has just set off with Elsie, her waters broke 10 minutes ago, and she wants her mum."

"I have waited so long for this moment, Dora, on our way."

"What now, Dora?"

"We wait, darling, and you being a patient man should have no problem with that?"

"What`s keeping her?"

Hahahaha

"Good afternoon, I have brought my wife, Elsie Davies, to have our first baby."

"Well, Sir, you have come to the right place. I am a Sister and run this shift of the baby factory. What are you both hoping for?"

"We truly do not mind, Sister."

"That is the very best way to be. Now then, Elsie, when was your last pain, my love?"

"Just as we were getting out of the car, Sister, and now, owwwwww."

"Perfect, let us get you into a gown and ready."

I followed up.

"You can sit there; we will call you when we need you."

"Oh, ok, Sister."

A few minutes later, Claire came in, and I kissed her cheek.

"Hello Claire, thank you for coming. I am afraid we are not allowed to go in."

"Hello Edward, are you ok?"

"Well, you know, nervous, I suppose."

"Is she in here?"

"Yes, but we have to stay here, please have my seat."

"Have to wait here, you say, I think not."

She knocked and walked in. Again, I went to follow.

"Did I call you lovey?"

"No but?"

"But?"

"But I think I will wait here."

"Good boy."

"Can I get you a cup of tea, Sir?"

"That would be lovely, thank you, nurse."

Hahaha

"As it happens, I am the hospital Matron."

"Did you get told to stay here, too?"

"Something like that, sugar?"

"Sugar, never been called that before, Matron."

"No, my love, would you like sugar in your tea?"

"Oh, sorry, my mind is scrambled."

"Just as it should be lovely."

She went away and came back with my tea and two biscuits.

"Thank you, Matron."

I must have sat for over an hour, and Sister came out, and I stood up.

"Nothing doing at the moment, you can go in if you wish."

"Yes, please, thank you."

"She is doing well, Edward, all going to plan."

"Thank you, Claire, you in pain love?"

"No, not at all, Edward, just the waiting I am not very good at."

"Spoilt by her dad as a child, that`s why Edward."

"I guessed so, but then again, she is so worth it."

"I am here, you know, you two?"

"Well, I love you so much, spoilt or not."

I saw her grimace.

"Owwwwww."

She gripped my hand.

"I am here for you, love, not sure for how long, minst!"

"Sister says that I am in good hands."

"Guess who made me a cup of tea?"

"No idea, Matron?"

"How the bejabbers did you know that?"

"Woman's, owwwwwww, intuition."

Sister came back in and checked under the covers.

"Would you like to go back to your seat outside, Sir?"

Now, was she asking me or telling me?

Her opening the door answered my question.

"Tea, one sugar, Sir?"

"That would be lovely, thank you."

"Do stop pacing up and down, Dora, and checking the phone is working will not get us a grandchild any sooner."

"I know, darling, how come you are so calm?"

"Army training. Dora, I could be sick with worry."

"Oh, my darling, you are human."

"Cup of tea, love?"

"Any Port left from Christmas, Dora?"

"Perhaps a little, shall we have it now or wait to toast our new grandchild?"

"Wait, I guess, so tea, please."

"That`s right, Elsie, push with the contraction, you are doing wonderfully well."

"Please can Edward come in, pleaseee."

"It is not usual, but I see it is distressing you, and you have enough to think about without the addition of stress."

"Thank you, Sister."

Sister walked to the door and opened it for me.

"Your presence is requested, Sir, not my choice, but who am I to have an opinion?"

"You are probably the best person in the whole world I would want with my wife, so if you wish, I will decline your kind offer."

"You are a complete gentleman; the respect you showed me just then has earned you a free pass. Please follow me, Sir."

I held one hand, and Caire held her other hand, and within about 10 minutes, Elie's last push had the desired effect.

Chapter 10

OUR FUTURE

Whilst our grandchild was being born, Martin took a funny turn right in front of my eyes. He just collapsed, and I was so shocked that he was getting up before I could get to him.

"Whatever happened then, Martin?"

"I must have tripped, it`s ok, Dora, don`t fuss."

"Good girl, that's it—just one last push, push, there, done.

I am so pleased to pass you your new baby, a sweet little BOY."

I rang home

"Hello Mum, you and Dad have a brand new grandson."

"Born when?"

"Less than 20 minutes ago."

"Weight?"

"Not long, mum, she was pretty quick."

"Darling, what weight was our grandson?"

"Oh, sorry, 7 pounds 7 ounces."

"Name?"

"Not been told yet!"

"Ok, darling, see you when you get home, give everyone our love."

"Will do, mum."

"About time we had some fantastic news, Dora, and that sure was fantastic news."

"Mum and Dad send all their love."

"I will leave you now, Elsie and get home to your dad."

"Ok, mum, have you come in your car?"

"Yes, I did love."

"Thanks for coming, mum, I really needed you. Send our love to Dad."

"I will walk you to your car, Claire. It is dark outside."

"Thank you, Edward, you are a right gentleman."

The Sister came back in as I was leaving.

"Right, Elsie, let's get you washed, into a nighty and into a proper bed."

"Thank you, Sister."

I took her mum to her car and kissed her cheek, and cuddled her.

"Ah, you are back; Sister is just getting your wife comfortable and ready to give the baby his first feed."

"Thank you, Matron."

I went to the bathroom to go to the loo and freshen up; all that tea was taking its toll.

"Ah, there you are, Mr Davies, follow me and I will take you to your family."

She opened the door, and I was shown in.

My eyes filled with tears. Elsie was sitting up in bed, breastfeeding our newborn son; it was a beautiful sight.

"Listen, Edward."

I could hear our baby sucking and grunting, accompanied by the snuffling of his little, blocked-up nose - priceless times.

"I have an idea of a name, Elsie."

"Me too, as it happens."

"Ok, if you say the first letter and I will say the last, ready?"

"Yes."

"After 3, 1 – 2 – 3."

"B."

"N."

"Not your dad`s name, Brian?"

"Yes."

I hugged her and our Brian.

"I thought he looked like Brian, and if he grows up like your dad, he will be a lovely man."

"Thank you, Edward, that was lovely."

Elsie and Brian came home after a five-day stay in the hospital, and we met our very new grandson. As soon as they arrived, Elsie put him into my arms. What a special and magical time for me.

Our lives soon fell into a routine, and I helped out whenever I was asked. I could not get enough of him. What is it about a newborn baby's chubby legs?

Elisabeth was worse than I and loved to be here for a cuddle. He was such an easy baby, always full of smiles and blowing bubbles.

He drank when she fed him, he burped when he was winded, slept when he was swaddled, and just lay on a mat and amused himself.

During the second month at home, Elsie would feed him at 10.00 pm and wake him again at 6.00 am.

He slept in a crib in their room; they only had one bedroom, which was okay for now, but would it mean they would move away into a bigger home in the future? I prayed for a miracle to keep them here.

The weeks flew by, and Elsie would be back at work next Monday, so she was sorting out babysitting duties between me, Claire, her mum, and herself, as she would now only work on Mondays, Wednesdays, and Fridays.

It worked perfectly. When it was my turn, I had the added help of Elizabeth, who was an absolute pleasure to entertain.

Christmas 1948 and Brian`s first visit from Santa Claus.

"I wonder what you would wish for if you could speak, little man. That was someone at our door, Brian. Oh, hello Paul, what a surprise."

"We are after a favour."

"Anything, Paul,"

"Anything?"

"Yes, for sure."

Could you find a home for this stray?"

"Laura."

Laura popped up from behind Paul.

"Merry Christmas, Brian, this is Peggy."

They put the dog inside the door and left.

"Now look what you have done, Brian Daniels, gone and got us a pet, and a beautiful little dog he is."

I put Brian on the floor, and with him just nicely crawling, he crawled over to Peggy, who licked his face, and that was it, friends for life.

We knew Brian would be safe with the chocolate brown Labrador.

Another knock on the door and they brought a steel dog crate, a basket, a litter tray and puppy food.

"Here is Peggy`s pedigree, and as you can see, Elsie, she goes back to your old Peggy and beyond, so she is a direct descendant."

"Thank you, Paul and Laura. I did not want another dog after our heartbreak of losing Peggy. But I love Brian`s present, she is adorable."

"She is 10 weeks old, she was born on 21st October and has two sisters and a brother, only the boy was golden, all the rest were Chocolate."

After our chat, I closed the door. Brian was asleep on the floor in front of our log fire, and Peggy was curled up right beside him.

"Hey, you two, quick, look at this."

I had to share the moment with them.

"As you said, Elsie, friends for life."

When Edward came home, he was met by a tipply toptail bundle of fluff. Peggy had not quite mastered the art of running without the falling skill.

In early 1949, Martin and Edward had letters from the General's Solicitors.

"You have a letter from a solicitor, Martin."

"Thank you, what a posh envelope."

Dear Mr. Davies

You are invited to the will-reading of the late General Edward Cartwright to be held at

Hareclough House on the 18th January 1949 at 10.00 am.

Yours sincerely

Eccleston's and Partners

"Well, I did not expect that. I wonder why me."

"Well, darling, you did save the General's life!"

"Though I did not do it to be rewarded."

"I know, I was not meaning that love"

Elsie gave Edward his envelope, and she said the conversation went much like ours.

It was the day of the will reading.

Tuesday, January 18th, 1949

"Thank you for meeting me today to read the last will of the late Field Marshal Edward Cartwright.

Notwithstanding, the whole estate now falls to my darling wife, Elisabeth May Cartwright.

I will go through the minor bequests at the end of my reading.

Hmm(He cleared his throat.)

To my saviour and truly one of our best friends, Captain Martin Daniels VC and to his son, my namesake and also my best friend, Lieutenant Edward Daniel, VC, I leave each 1 Acre of land on the lower 9 acres, overlooking the memory beach and river Tauper.

On this land, they can build the house of their dreams, to which I bequeath them £7,500 each.

To Paul Daniels, another close friend, for mentoring all the children on our estate, lifelong free rent to the gamekeepers' house, when it becomes available, plus £2,500 for him to use as he wishes.

As for...............

We left Hareclough House, unsure if we were stunned, maybe shocked, or perhaps astounded, but happy and respectful of a great man's memory.

We went down to our land and just stood looking at the mighty Tauper River. We knew that one day, very soon, we would be living there, so much to decide on style and rooms. Luckily, we have two who know exactly what they want: Dora and Elsie, so the job was left to them.

Dad had said no hurry, but as soon as possible.

"A little gossip, Elsie."

"Oh, do tell."

"Paul asked if Laura could sleep over last night."

"And?"

"Well, his dad had a quiet word with him about you know what."

"Wow, what did he say about that?"

"He said Laura was not his first girlfriend and he had ample protection in his bedside drawer."

"How sweet, so it is pretty serious?"

"I do hope so at 33, he should be."

"How old is Laura?"

"24/25 I think."

"Maybe wedding bells soon, wouldn`t that be nice?"

Within a year, everything was decided on the houses. Work started in the late summer of 1950.

"So, what have we finally decided to do, Martin?"

"Well, Edward and I agree we want two separate houses, not joined on, and I think you two are happy with that, right, Dora?"

"Yes, Martin, that would be nice."

"We will have them built out of reclaimed stone, to fit in with the surrounding buildings on the estate, agreed?"

"Yes, for sure we both love the look and warmth of proper stone."

"We all think identically inside with a large kitchen, big enough to have a dining table in."

"And a huge log-fired range for cooking and getting the water hot as well as heating a lot of the house."

"Yes, agreed, a nice-sized family lounge with a big log fireplace and to complete downstairs, a formal dining room to be used for whatever, just a spare room, also with a fireplace.

"Maybe a laundry room downstairs, Martin, and a large cold pantry, and also maybe a toilet and wash basin?"

"Good idea, I will have those added."

"Upstairs, a bath and shower room, two double bedrooms and a larger bedroom for us."

"Maybe a toilet connected to the main bedroom, Martin?"

"That is novel, my dear, but let's see what can be done."

"Oops."

"You ok, Martin?"

"Yes, I tripped over my shoes, just clumsy."

I thought that was the second trip/fall in a few months.

"I cannot believe we will be in our new home well before Christmas, Edward. I thought it would take a couple of years to build what we wanted?"

"Me neither, Elsie. We can have your parents stay for Christmas and even sleep over.

"That would be lovely, thank you. Do you have any idea how much we have spent on our new home so far?

"I know exactly, Elsie, £ 2,149 with another £300 for internal fittings, kitchen, bathroom, flooring, etc. You can go into town and choose everything we need to furnish, bedding and linen."

"What would you like your bedroom to be like, Brian?"

"Please may I have a bed and curtains, mummy?"

"Of course you can love."

Brian, my mum, Dora, and Elisabeth set off one morning to the nearest City with a furniture store.

I had made an appointment with the manager regarding our visit.

"Good morning, Mr Bishop, we are here to hopefully buy furniture for our two, three-bedroomed houses and wondered what sort of deal he would give us, as in a discount."

"Well, Mrs Daniels, how does 20% off everything and free delivery?"

"Sounds a lot better than ever I expected, thank you."

"I will also throw in a personal shopping assistant who will guide you throughout the store and write down all you buy."

Thank you."

"Please, follow me."

We went onto the shop floor and were introduced to Hazel, who would be our guide.

We bought everything you could think of, from a toothbrush to a dining table. We did not need wardrobes, as they were built into each bedroom.

At lunchtime, we went into the restaurant and even got 20% off.

We bought our last items at 3.30 pm and went for a coffee.

The total invoice for me was £420, minus the 20% discount, which was £336. For my mum, the total was £405, minus the 20% discount, which was £324.

Dora paid for both by cheque and gave our address, 1 Hareclough House Cottage and for us, 2 Hareclough House Cottage.

"Thank you very much, Mr Bishop, we will confirm the delivery date 2 weeks before we need it, if that is ok?"

"That would be perfect, thank you, ladies, safe journey home."

Brian was asleep all the way home, as were Dora and Elisabeth.

We have all never felt so tired of spending money.

We wrote down the things we had not ordered, such as an egg timer and alarm clock - little things, but still important.

We never told anyone, but Martin has collapsed on the floor two or three times, dizzy, breathless and feeling really fatigued.

I made him an appointment at the doctor's and went with him.

"Good morning, Mr Daniels, not sure we have met before, and I have been here 15 years or more, so you have been pretty well. How can I help you today?"

Martin explained his recent falls and the total lack of energy he has experienced over the past couple of months.

The doctor gave him a full shirt and vest from medical supplies and took several vials of blood from him.

He listened to his heart and lungs, took his temperature and blood pressure, and even had him sit on the edge of the bed to test his reflexes.

"These blood tests should be back within the week, and the secretary will contact you with an appointment when we have them."

"Thank you, doctor. Should he do anything in particular, doctor?"

"Anything you feel like, but no excursion."

"Thank you, doctor. See you next week.

It was my day for Brian and his best mate, Peggy. As if having a baby wasn't spoiling me enough, Peggy was double-spoiling me.

We went for a walk down to the river, which was only five minutes away. Brian was in his pram, and Peggy was on a lead, walking most beautifully.

I dare not let her off, other animals about, and how could I tell Elsie and Edward I had lost their dog?

It was a lovely day, so Brian and Peggy dug holes on the beach. He laughed, she wagged her tail, two more than happy babies.

I took them both a drink and a rusk for Brian and dog biscuits for Peggy.

As promised, the doctor's secretary rang and made us an appointment for the following day.

Not that Martin was one to complain about anything, but this was different.

Martin has been run down and listless over the past few weeks, not the health of a typical 57-year-old.

"Come in, Mr and Mrs Daniels, I have all the results from your tests, and I am afraid I have no good news."

I held Martin's hand tightly.

"Your symptoms of breathlessness, always tired, a cough you cannot shift, are the result of you having Acute Heart failure."

I could not help but sob, brave Captain Daniels VC, too.

He gave us a few minutes to regain our composure.

"Basically, your heart is not strong enough to pump your blood around your body to fulfil all its needs. The hard part for you, Martin, is that it cannot be stopped or slowed down."

"Can we do anything at all to gain time, Doctor?"

"Just take it easy and sit with the odd walk. I am so sorry."

"Could we have an end prognosis at all, Doctor?"

"All I could offer is to take it day by day. If you died from Heart Failure, it would be a steady decline in health to the end. If you kept busy, a heart Attack could kill you. I am so sorry."

"Thank you for being so candid, doctor, no way the news we wanted, but news we accept from you."

Martin shook the doctor's hand, and we emerged in a daze, needing time to digest it.

Our moving-in day was pretty special. Claire and Brian came down to help Elsie and Edward, and we had Paul, Laura, and Elisabeth to assist us, with Martin in a supervisory capacity.

Outside was still to finish off with fencing and a few outbuildings for Edward and a few kennels for us, although the leading kennels would remain with Paul at the gamekeeper's house.

We had a joint housewarming party at both our houses.

Martin clinked a spoon against his glass to get everyone's attention.

"Ladies and gentlemen, thank you so much for attending our joint housewarming party. May I propose a toast, please? The toast is to absent friends."

"Absent Friends."

"Now, on a personal level, news from me. As you are aware, I have been undergoing treatment for various conditions over the past year or so. I have spoken to my employer, Elisabeth, and have decided to retire, passing on the Estate Managers post to my son, Paul. I will tidy up the rough edges and hope to finish in a week or so, thank you."

"Ladies and gentlemen, a toast, the toast is my dad, Martin Danniels."

"Martin Daniels."

The party was an excellent event, and when everyone but my family had gone home, I spoke to my family.

"It may have been a shock to you all, but I am seriously ill, I am afraid. I have Heart Failure, and the doctor told me to enjoy every day as if it were my last, as very soon, it will be."

Mum and Dad began to cry, as did all of us; he was the leader of the pack, the one who was always there, and his news shattered us.

Dad got gradually worse, first by the week and then by the day.

"Edward, your dad wants us all in his room. Paul is on his way."

He was propped up on his pillow and looked very pale. He managed to speak very softly.

"Thank you all for coming, but I feel it only right and proper to give you all an update I got from the Doctor!"

"He said when he examined him, he could tell his body was beginning to close down and be prepared for the worst, very soon."

My mum cried, and I tried to comfort her.

"Dora."

Dad held out his arm, the best he could and held her hand and took a deep breath; it was to be his last.

Hareclough Heights

Hareclough Heights

Chapter 11

JUST SURVIVING

I could feel Martin`s soul pass through me. I looked up, and there he was, floating away from us all. He smiled as he disappeared into the clouds.

We were all crying, and rightly so; he had earned that as a right the way he had fought in two wars and came back to look after us.

I would have followed him in a heartbeat had it been possible. Everyone left as I waited for the ambulance to come and take his body away from me.

The doctor came to certify him dead, and they took him away in the ambulance. I watched it go out of sight. I was heartbroken

I was alone in a new house with a million rooms, yet not one memory. However, was I going to survive this dreadful time all alone in the world?

"Mum?"

"In our bedroom, coming."

It was Elsie.

"Do you want to sleep in our house for a while?"

"No, thank you, I need some time on my own."

"How about a bit of company for a few days with Peggy?"

"Oh, thank you, Elsie."

"She is nearly house-trained but has good manners."

"I know she has Elsie."

"I was talking to Peggy's mum."

I laughed through my tears.

"Won't Brian miss him?"

"He will be here tomorrow to be looked after, if you still want him."

"Oh, yes, please."

She kissed me and said goodnight. I went back to our bedroom, and Peggy jumped up and lay on Martin`s side.

"Clever girl."

The next few days were about survival, and now, as head of this family, I had to show I was strong. I either cried alone or when I had Peggy with me.

Edward and Paul asked if it was ok for them to organize the funeral. I said it was fine, and when all was organized, they came to tell me what I needed to know and when.

I stayed in with Peggy, wandering from room to room.

"Next Friday, mum, and as dad had won the VC, the army is organizing it all, if that is ok with you?"

"Yes, he deserves that, thank you, boys."

I got through the pomp and ceremony that a VC winner deserves, and sat through the wake and handshaking, not for me, but for Martin. I felt him by my side all day.

When I was brought home, he spoke to me.

"Goodbye now, Dora, this is where I have to leave you. I want you to be strong for our family. You are the Matriarch; they will all look to you for guidance. During the week, I want you to sort all my clothes out and ask Paul if he would take them to the homeless shop, not the uniforms."

"What would you like me to do with them, love, Martin, Martin...."

I was too late; he had gone, but never, ever, forgotten.

After I had been home for a few hours, Paul and Laura called.

"We need your help, mum. This is her last pup, a real runt, and her mom will not let her feed. Could you look after her, or shall I get a bucket of water?"

"You will do no such thing. Pass it here. Did you bring any formula down? Yes, in my car, I will get it."

Laura cuddled me as I cuddled the pup.

"I put it in the kitchen with a bottle, every four hours, mum. What can you call her? We already have a Peggy next door?"

"She will be known as pup, Paul, and thank you."

She was just what I needed, and over the next few days, Paul and Laura brought me a steel cage and bedding. They also got a litter tray when they brought Pup.

I had Brian and Peggy the day after, and although I was short on sleep, I had Elisabeth, a very regular caller, with me.

"You really have your hands full today, Dora."

"Yes, I would not want it any other way. Have you met Pup?"

"She is tiny, cute, and I love her."

She began to squeak.

"Would you like to feed her, Elisabeth?"

"Yes, please, Dora, how often do you feed her?"

"Every 4 hours, 6 times a day, then into her tray, she goes to the toilet, back into her bed, and we start again every 4 hours.

"You must be shattered?"

"Yep, but I love her so much, Elisabeth."

"Easy to see why, would you like me to come and stay a while and help with the evening feeds?"

I would not say it was part of my plan in life to integrate Elisabeth into more of our lives, as I am not at all conceited, but it was!

"That would be so lovely of you, Elisabeth. Thank you for the offer."

"Shall I pop up for a few overnight items now?"

"Yes, please and get someone to carry it down."

"I will, a good idea, Dora, thank you."

We got on really, really well and carried our closeness past weaning a puppy, but as months flew by, so did the years.

Elisabeth became unwell and collapsed on her way to see me. She was not found until hours later and never survived it.

It was another setback in my life, but I had to realize she was 88 years old, and I like to think we both spent a lovely time growing old together. I was now 77 years old.

Brian loved his schooling and always had top marks, not because his two teacher parents brainwashed him; he was just very bright and inquisitive.

It served him well, and he is now training to become a solicitor; he was taken on by a big firm in town a few years ago.

I will let Elsie tell you about him. I hope she tells you she is on Peggy number 3 now, and I am on Pup number two, who is now 11 years old, bless her, not a moment's trouble.

Our Brian has made a beautiful young man, with all the looks of his dad and granddad and has a lovely girlfriend in Alice. They met at college; she is also studying law, in a different sphere, I think.

Dora was about the same age; Edward and I are racing towards 60, or so it seems, as time flies so quickly.

"It will soon be Christmas, Edward, and this year we will probably be only the 2, your mum, my mum and dad."

"Has Brian said he won't be joining us?"

"Just surmising, he was with us last year, and Alice will probably want to spend it with her mum; it upsets me a lot, but it cannot be helped."

"Then invite her mum too, we have the room, here and mums."

"Do you really think we would have enough bedrooms? Shall we go and count them, Edward, and maybe try one or two for size?"

"Sounds like a good plan if we take it slowly."

"A good day at work, Brian?"

"Yes, thanks mum, I love all the different jobs, law, conveyancing, will writing, such a great mixture. What`s for tea, Mum?"

"Meat and potato pie with squashy peas."

"My favourite."

"Everything is your favourite."

"Yes, true, apart from fish."

"Ah, yes, apart from fish."

"Hello, you two."

I put my arms around Edward's neck and kissed him.

"Hello, my darling boy, did you have a good day in class?"

"Yes, wonderful, thank you, tea smells delicious."

"Sorry, I am late. I nodded off."

"No problem, mum."

We all sat down to eat.

"Brian, if Alice`s mum may be at her home this Christmas, please invite her here, for Boxing Day too, if she wants, he can stop over."

"Oh, wow, Dad, Mum, what a lovely thing to offer, thank you."

"We do not like to think people are alone at Christmas."

"In that case, can Alice stay with me?"

"Of course, son, if you are sensible?"

"Oh, we are, Sir."

"Are, son?"

"Busted."

Hahahahaha

I have two spare rooms, Edward, if needed."

"You mum, we may need two rooms, one for Martin and one for Alice."

"Aww, Dad."

"Edward, stop teasing."

"Sorry, mum."

Edward and I cleared away, Brian went to his room, and Mum went home.

"Our plan looks to have worked, Edward."

"Not really a plan, we do not like to think of people alone at any time, let alone at

Christmas, after having so many away from home."

"I agree, love."

Alice was so happy with our suggestion, and she and her mum came for Christmas Day and Boxing Day.

It was easier all round that Brian and Alice slept next door; I'm not sure what Alice's mum, May Happs, would make of it.

Christmas 1972 was a huge success all around, and we asked everyone to stay on Boxing Day night as well.

"I will make a big breakfast and put it on the table, so help yourself.

"Brian, was your grandma up when you left? I feel her mind is letting her down. Last night she said she will go now, Martin is waiting for her?"

"She was up later, so I went to see if she was ok. She said she had indigestion and was waiting till it eased."

Everyone ate and left.

"You have a funny feeling, too, Edward."

"Yes, you too, hey, will you come round with me?"

"Of course."

We went in and called.

Edward knocked on her bedroom door.

"You ok, mum??

We went in, and she was lying motionless in bed and cuddling a photo of my dad. I just burst into tears, and Elsie too.

I sat and held her freezing-cold hand, and Elsie and I said a prayer for her.

"It was not her mind letting her down; she was right, Dad was waiting for her.

I rang Pul and an ambulance. Paul was close and came straight down, and we all waited for the doctor and ambulance staff.

The doctor pronounced her dead, and she was taken to the hospital.

We went back to our house, and I made us a cup of tea.

A week later, we had a beautiful funeral for Dora, attended by family and friends, and even an army General who knew our family was present.

We will never forget the ones we loved and have lost, but real life must carry on.

Brian and Alice planned their wedding for Valentine's Day 1972 and had agreed to rent what was now Paul's house at a very low rent.

It was not long before Alice fell pregnant and gave us all a lovely event to look forward to.

She gave birth on Valentine's Day 1974 to a little boy and named him after his grandad, Martin.

Edward and I were extremely proud grandparents and worshipped our little boy.

We had everything ready for them both when they came home. Edward had painted and papered Martin`s bedroom with blue paint and nursery rhyme wallpaper. They had a crib, and I had already embroidered two sets of bedding and blankets, along with hats and cardigans, and a baby grow that I had bought.

When we visited them in the hospital, I donated all the pink items to them; they were very grateful, saying they had very little to dress babies in when needed for parents with limited financial means.

That gave me an idea. I was a member of a Tuesday group that met weekly to discuss the world's problems. A few weeks ago, someone said it is a shame we are not more productive instead of just nattering.

I have an answer to our nonproductive chat: how about knitting as we natter? I explained the hospital's woes, and so our knitting group, which had formed within a group, was established. We now supply every hospital in town, and the Mothers' Union groups have also adopted our idea.

I helped Alice with Martin in those early years, but only when asked. It is different when it is your daughter; the bond is closer, so instead of just turning up next door, she came to me, and regularly too.

Great-uncle Paul managed to find a puppy that no one else wanted. I think you're familiar with the story and its outcome. Martin and Peggy grew up together; he would sit on the little chairs, and Peggy would chew on the legs of the chair as he sat on it.

No one seemed to mind, and we just bought again what had been chewed. Alice never wanted her in a cage. She was not that bad; who am I trying to kid? She had a chew at absolutely everything.

Like all Labradors, particularly the chocolate brown ones, they had such an understanding nature. Okay, maybe the "don't chew" gene was missing from Peggs, but on the whole, Martin and Peggy were best friends.

As time passed, we all grew a bit older. I had now been retired for several years, and Edward retired at 65. Martin lost his best friend, Peggy, but as luck would have it, Uncle Paul found an immediate replacement.

We were now fortunate enough to be living with a generation that wanted little in life but got a lot, and hire purchase was king, as they wanted it now, so how much could they afford a week?

Not sure if I agreed with it, but Edward and I sure like the easy way of life and mobile phones, who would have thought it possible."

I think that's about it for my past family, and the only ones still with us are my granddad, Edward; Grandma, Elsie; Uncle Paul; and Aunty Laura.

Granddad and Grandma live in the house next door to us, which is where my dad, Brian, and I, Martin, and my mum, Alice, live. Oh, and Peggy, my chocolate brown Labrador, is continuing the family tradition of chewing anything.

I have just finished my A levels and achieved well, with many passes that will help me secure a place at university if I wish to do so. I don't want it, and Uncle John said that if Mum and Dad said it was okay, I could become his apprentice estate manager and gamekeeper.

We all agreed, and I will start following on Monday. I have worked Saturdays and Sundays, and in the summer after school, for Uncle Paul, so I am pretty familiar with the basics.

"Have you everything ready for tomorrow, Martin?"

"I think so, Mum, do you mean workwear?"

"Yes, and morning snack and lunch?"

"Never gave that a thought."

"One of us has, fortunately."

"Thanks, mum."

I set my phone alarm for 6:30, but I was in the shower at 6:00.

Dressed, breakfast and up at Uncle John`s for just after 7.00

He saw me outside and called me in.

"Early Bird."

"I have always got up early, Uncle Paul."

"This is your first lesson, call me Paul."

"I will try, won`t be easy after 18 years."

"I know, son."

"I managed to get you on a day release for the Estate Management side of your apprenticeship."

"Thank you, I really do appreciate your help, Sir."

"We are family, Martin."

"Yes, I am fortunate to have you and Aunty Laura and all these beautiful dogs."

"And all related to Martin."

"How so?"

"So, we are keeping the breeding line to give us more chocolate than yellow or black, and their good nature, like Peggy."

I had an excellent week working with Uncle Paul, but at last it was Friday, and I was meeting my girlfriend, Amy.

"Are you and Amy going out tonight, Martin?"

"Yes, mum, just to Tinkers with Andy, Billy and partners. Is it ok for Amy to sleep over?"

"Yes, of course, love, thanks for asking."

Martin had been with Amy since school, and both Edward and I like her a lot. They have slept together for over a year now, and it is no problem for us at all.

They were embarrassed when I said her mum had to ring me to confirm she was happy with the arrangement. Her parents were like us; they were delighted and asked about their relationship.

"What would you like to drink, Amy?"

"Lemonade, please."

"2 Lemonades with ice, please, Peter."

"You 2 doing ok?"

"Yes, thanks, you and Bryony?"

"Yes, thanks, the same."

He waved at Amy.

Our friends joined us, and we stayed all evening, dancing to the live group they had on.

It was a great evening; we said goodbye to our friends and took a taxi home around 10:30.

Mum and Dad were still up, and we had had a bedtime hot chocolate and petted Peggy.

"A good night, Martin?"

"Yes, very, the group were great."

"We had not seen them before, and they were excellent."

"So, you're sort of music then, Amy.

?"

"Very much so, Mrs Daniels, a lot of covers and one or two of their own stuff."

"Oh, good, you can call me Alice if you wish."

"And maybe mum when we get married."

Martin stood up and stood Amy up.

He knelt on one knee..

"Amy Brookes, will you marry me?"

"Oh yes, Martin."

He took a box out of his pocket with his Grandmas engagement ring and slipped it on her finger.

He stood up and kissed and cuddled, and we stood up and kissed and cuddled them.

So we were not still up after 10:00 to welcome them home. Martin had asked for our permission, as he had asked Mr. and Mrs. Brookes during the week.

We went to bed first, and they washed up and put the mugs away.

"When did you plan all this, Martin Daniels?"

"A few weeks ago, I asked mum and dad, and mum said I could have her mum's engagement ring, and I asked your parent last week when you were at night school."

"No way would I have said no, Martin; I love you so much."

"Probably as much as I love you, Amy."

"I have been doing our family tree, and do you know my grandad was in the army during the war and was away from 1914 to 1918 and then again from 1939 to 1945, so they were apart 10 years out of their married life."

"That in itself must have been unbearable; he should have got a medal."

"He did not do too badly on he medal front, and when he passed, he left me them and I wear them at the cenotaph every Remembrance Day. I am so proud of him."

"I think you may have spilled on your shirt, my darling. Let's go take it off."

"After you, Amy."

Amy and I were fortunate in our lives; we both had parents, and we both had grandparents who were still alive.

We wanted to build a life together that surrounded us with loved ones.

On Saturday morning, we took Peggy and walked hand in hand up to the top of Hareclough Hill, looking down at our valley. Does this sound familiar?

****